PRIDE

7 Deadly Sins Vol. 7

First published as a collection May 2019
Content copyright © Pure Slush Books and individual authors
Edited by Matt Potter

BP#00079

All rights reserved by the authors and publisher. Except for brief excerpts used for review or scholarly purposes, no part of this book may be reproduced in any manner whatsoever without express written consent of the publisher or the author/s.

Pure Slush Books
32 Meredith Street
Sefton Park SA 5083
Australia

Email: edpureslush@live.com.au
Website: https://pureslush.com/
Store: https://pureslush.com/store/

Original peacock image copyright © SilviaP_Design
Cover design copyright © Matt Potter

ISBN: 978-1-925536-72-0

Also available as an eBook
ISBN: 978-1-925536-73-7

A note on differences in punctuation and spelling

Pure Slush Books proudly features writers from all over the English-speaking world. Some speak and write English as their first language, while for others, it's their second or third or even fourth language. Naturally, across all versions of English, there are differences in punctuation and spelling, and even in meaning. These differences are reflected in the work *Pure Slush Books* publishes, and they account for any differences in punctuation, spelling and meaning found within these pages.

Pure Slush Books is a member of the
Bequem Publishing collective
http://www.bequempublishing.com/

• RubinA • Sara ABEND-SIMS • Annabelle BAPTISTA • Paul BECKMAN • Jim BELL • Henry BLADON • John BOST • Howard BROWN • William BUTLER • Elizabeth BUTTIMER • Steve CARR • Guilie CASTILLO ORIARD • Con CHAPMAN • Chuka Susan CHESNEY • Jan CHRONISTER • Robert COOPERMAN • Mark CRIMMINS • Steve CUSHMAN • Tony DALY • Sue DAWES • Ruth Z. DEMING • Albert DeGENOVA • Steven DEUTSCH • Michael ESTABROOK • Tom FEGAN • Nod GHOSH • Ken GOSSE • Shane GUTHRIE • Chris HALL • Sarah HENRY • Jo HOCKING • Ryn HOLMES • Mark HUDSON • Dawid JURASZEK • Jemshed KHAN • Norman KLEIN • Eddy KNIGHT • Mary KRAKOW • Len KUNTZ • Bruce LADER • Ron. LAVALETTE • Larry LEFKOWITZ • Cynthia LESLIE-BOLE • Lia LEWIS • Mike LEWIS-BECK • Peter LINGARD • JP LUNDSTROM • Jan McCARTHY • Karla Linn MERRIFIELD • Peter MICHAL • Marsha MITTMAN • Colleen MOYNE • Piet NIEUWLAND • Pat O'CONNOR • Carl 'Papa' PALMER • Beatrice PRETI • Felix PURAT • Anna PURVES • Aaron RETZ • Chad ROHRBACHER • Ruth Sabath ROSENTHAL • Ed RUZICKA • Gerard SARNAT • R Scott SEXTON • Cormac STAGG • Joseph STEARMAN • Lisa STICE • Duncan STRACHAN • Margaret SWART • Charles David TAYLOR • Lucy TYRRELL • Emery VEILLEUX •

Contents

1   Poetry

71   Prose

Poetry

5	This One is Mine	*Lisa Stice*
6	To Be Tough	*Tony Daly*
7	Reviewing the Situation	*John Bost*
8	Cold is Deeper Than Pride	*Lucy Tyrrell*
9	With as Much Pride as I Can Muster *Ruth Sabath Rosenthal*	
10	Beach Life	*Ryn Holmes*
11	Vitamin D	*Sarah Henry*
12	Hiraeth	*Steven Deutsch*
13	The Proud Homecoming King	*Mike Lewis-Beck*
14	The variety of human voting	*Piet Nieuwland*
16	The Cuckold	*Con Chapman*
18	Alexander	*Dawid Juraszek*
19	Backpedal? Just saying …	*Margaret Swart*
20	Truth be Told	*Bruce Lader*
21	Typing Lesson	*Carl 'Papa' Palmer*
22	When Cars Were America	*Ed Ruzicka*
24	Tedious	*Michael Estabrook*
25	Found on a Package of Frida Kahlo Socks *Jan Chronister*	
26	After Sunrise, All Is White	*R Scott Sexton*
27	Birthday in Bled	*Felix Purat*
28	The Fall	*Howard Brown*
29	Shame, Shame	*Ron. Lavalette*
30	Pride of Authorship	*Jemshed Khan*

32	The Simple Girl	*Colleen Moyne*
34	Annual Physical at 55	*Karla Linn Merrifield*
36	Even Steven	*Anna Purves*
38	The Drunken Cock	*Chad Rohrbacher*
40	Pride	*Cormac Stagg*
42	From Invincible to Invisible	*Mark Hudson*
45	Until Mama's Proud of Me	*Beatrice Preti*
46	Those Eyes, Those Damned Eyes	*William Butler*
48	The woman next to me	*Chuka Susan Chesney*
50	The "self-made" man	*Marsha Mittman*
52	An Acquired Taste—Or Not	*Elizabeth Buttimer*
54	His Rightful Place	*Sara Abend-Sims*
56	Coming of Age	*Gerard Sarnat*
58	Agamemnon Sets Sail from Troy, with Cassandra in Tow	*Robert Cooperman*
60	Brave Pride	*Albert DeGenova*
62	The Changing of the Guards Cometh After a Fall	*Ken Gosse*
64	Parental Echoes	*Shane Guthrie*
66	Bathroom Reading	*Emery Veilleux*

This One is Mine
after the Rifleman's Creed

Lisa Stice

There she is. The small one over
there with the awkward run that
every five-year-old has, but look
there how her backpack reaches
there to her knees, how she balances
there on one leg then quickly moves
there to pick up litter out of rocks while
I wait here in the car line and watch.
There are others like her (maybe), but
this one is mine. I am useless, it is
true, without her. She and I know
there was no time before her. And
she has a father. We teach her to
be clean and ready. And she has a
brother (who is a terrier). We are
there to teach how weaknesses can
be strengths, how small ones can be
there right next to everyone, or even
there somewhere ahead. We are a part
of each other. From here, I watch her
there. Look how she pulls everything
into her sights, ready to move from
there, clean into wherever she wants.

To Be Tough

Tony Daly

Retirement would bring freedom, you dreamed.
You'd do the things you couldn't, in uniform:
grow your hair long and a beard too,
tie yourself naked to the old oak tree,
take those illicit drugs you were never allowed:
LSD, cocaine, meth, maybe even marijuana.

We all took it as a joke, but still wondered.
After all, when you first put on those Navy bell bottoms,
you rolled an unopened pack of smokes in your
sleeve for no other reason than to look tough,
too proud to be seen as anything less than your mates.

Tough climbing a palm tree in the South China Sea in '72.
Tough falling, bleeding into the saltwater.
Tough after 9/11, deploying to dress the dead for burial.
Tough pinning ribbons on chests without shedding tears.
You believed you were tough, keeping your scars inside.
They only escaped at night as cries in the dark,
and running in your sleep.

Reviewing the Situation

John Bost

The group of editors met for their weekly lunch
Out on the deck, these cool cats gathered –
Their tawny-colored manes of hair blew
in the breeze, sandwiched between their words
Roars of laughter found occasion to be heard –
While they snacked on and shared morsels
Delectable tales of missing commas, incomplete sentences
Running on to misplaced verbs and dramatic dashes –
Appalling apostrophes making sudden appearances
What possessed them, they'd pause to wonder
To exclaim, mark their words in raucous red
Until they turned blue, saddened by the state of affairs
They tasked themselves to revise and to reveal –
Lines labored on late into early evenings
These editors talked and tirelessly tinkered
Once more doing the lion's share of the work
This pride of crafty creative and cool cats
Patiently pondered … paused, 'til all was fit to print.

Cold is Deeper Than Pride

Lucy Tyrrell

Driving to the library,
I see lavender-pink plumes
belch from industrial stacks
into pale eerie landscape

of minus thirty—ice fog,
car exhaust, distant mountains.
In the foyer, on a bench,
an unshaven man sits, bent—

head in hands, elbows on knees
of tattered pants. Sturdy brown
paper wraps his feet—rags tie
up the bulky creases, hold

rumpled folds over his toes.
While he dozes, I take his
photograph, feeling guilty—
at closing time, I'll go home.

With as Much Pride as I Can Muster

Ruth Sabath Rosenthal

This old heart of mine no longer beats
down the doldrums, nor turns humdrum
bright as gold, as it did in my prime;

and nightly, in dreams high in my vessel
of wanting delight, it's strangers acting
out *my* desires! Imagine that! Intruders

beating me to the punch in the quest for
hot sex: Moist bodies embrace, legs, twixt
& twain, heighten each twist & turn

of a lusty mind. And this morning I wake
far from alright, vowing to lotion my loins
daily, perfume my skin and, if my old man

again says, *Not tonight dear*, I'll write this
craft of mine, shove it in his face, and ride
out the current into the sunset

with as much pride as I can muster.

Beach Life

Ryn Holmes

The Gulf is gorgeous today:
a perfect emerald fading to azure
banded by the indigo of deep water.
Along the shore,
a sandpiper trills optimism.
A little scientist with needled beak,
its dead-eye sharp vision
probes for breakfast.

Tired of waiting,
restless juveniles take flight nearby,
chased off by an old bird
running low to the ground –
head thrust out,
back hunched,
wings folded back –
in profile, resembling a feathered,
fussy schoolmaster scolding unruly boys.
It's impatient with the squabble of gulls
trading local news up on the dune.

Obvious interloper:
black pigeon in birdy suit and tie
dressed too formally for pacing.
Smug, it gloats over a new prize –
slow death in a bright plastic package.

Vitamin D

Sarah Henry

Vitamin D is needed to maintain strong bones.
You can tell I'm a proud woman
by the way I carry myself.

Vitamin D hardens teeth.
So they present a united front.

Calcium plus D supplements prevent falls.
I have outlived my husband long enough
to discover the fountain of minerals.
I play golf and brag about my scores.

Exposure to sunlight is required for absorption.
If I were made of chlorophyll,
my leaves would spread wide open.

Milk is a good food source.
From the land to the cow to the farmer
to the truck to the store to my mouth
and liver and kidneys, the endless
chain is necessary, unlike the card
club I can quit any time I want.

Hiraeth

Steven Deutsch

Sure, Moses qualifies
but it's hardly a stretch
to include those
DNA ghouls—
lanced and shorn—
who purpose their lives
in finding
some fabulous
ancestor—
hoping they might puff
up their emaciated chests
like frigatebirds
in heat
and point excitedly to
an illustrious branch
of their family tree—
but seem, always,
to come up with
monkeys.

The Proud Homecoming King

Mike Lewis-Beck

The proud homecoming king

rides high, waves regal, from his football throne.
The fans toss their caps, wave back from the throng.

A fella in a letter-sweater salutes his chief.
Two teens in tight skirts toss pink daisies.

Senior Citizens in wheelchairs marvel
when he flexes—and flexes—to catch a phantom pass.

See the Queen, behind the King, her eyes turned
as she waves to the cute guy in the pork-pie

who waves back to her. Watch the King's
face frown while he grinds out a fake smile

just before he puts a paw too high up the Queen's waist.

The variety of human voting

Piet Nieuwland

It's the general election, and after a tumultuous campaign voting concludes on a Saturday in early spring. At the Anglican Hall as a scrutineer I sit behind several Electoral Officials. I'm there to ensure that there is no attempt to influence the voters' decisions. It's a big steep high roofed hall with mirrors along the back wall. Who votes?
A man with one leg on crutches
A woman in a wheelchair
Another woman in a wheelchair
A man with three children who declares he is voting green, both party and candidate votes
A man whose orange shirt declares 'go fuck yourself'
A proud tall young woman who smiles a huge grin at me as she strides in, and out of the hall
A man whom I know asks how I am. I reply 'I can't really talk now'
A woman whom I've recently met sits down, asks me for my phone number, then walks away blushing saying 'Oh gosh, how embarrassing'
A woman who looks like a fashion model with a child in rainbow dress

A young Indian couple beaming
The smiling officials greet each voter, issue instructions, tear voting papers from the block and fold them, ask for the voters card, clarify name and address
Officials at the special votes booth are busy, lots of people are voting outside their electorate. It looks complicated sometimes.
A scrutineer from another party, the opposition blues looks on, an unfriendly sneer
The people who ask, I haven't done a tick, just a mark, is that ok?
The woman who returns in a fluster exclaiming 'I think I left my Ipad in the booth, is it there?' It is.
Another leaves their glasses
Some people give nothing away
People not on a roll, go over there

The Cuckold

Con Chapman

The train is late, and so I stop to talk
  with my son's old hockey coach.
We chat of this and that and
  after a while he breaks it off
  at another man's approach.

I know the newcomer too, but we do
  not speak. I had dinner with him once
  years ago, we have sons the same age.
My family moved and we lost touch;
  in the vogue phrase, we turned the page.

It was an uncomfortable Thanksgiving, I recall;
  his ancestors' portraits lined the walls
  in the dining room and the halls.
Later, my wife told me the reason
  for the tense knot in the evening—

  his wife had made love to another man,
  out of spite or lust or to wake him from
  his slumber of convention, we never learned.
We were there as a foil, a first step
  towards reconciliation, unction and oil.

We may have helped,
   or at least didn't hurt.
We bridged the silence that would
   otherwise have been there. We did what
   we could between the soup and dessert.

The cuckoo lays her egg in the nest of another
   mother, first pushing out one of that bird's
   eggs. The egg of the cuckoo matches the one
   displaced in a mimetic fall from grace.

When the young cuckoo is hatched, it
   works its back against all else in the nest,
   eggs or chicks. It gives them a push,
   causing them to fall, to die on the ground below.

I wondered if the look in the fellow's eye,
   avoiding my gaze, laughing at his own
   jokes, staring off into the distance,
   was caused by that sort of blow.

Alexander

Dawid Juraszek

A stirring story under his pillow
he warred on distant lands
to rule the ends of the world

Drunk on his own name
he scorched restless roads
through silence and shade

Looking up to his gods
he fantasized of immortality
earthly bounds be damned

Not stopped by his people
he would have sunk the sun itself
in the outer seas

Not undone by his flaws
he would have drenched the dead
in the tears of survivors

Not ended by his fever
he would have drowned multitudes
in their own blood

And then died anyway.

Backpedal? Just saying ...

Margaret Swart

I'm wrong
So don't try to convince me that
I know what I'm talking about
I'd deny my phobia of truth
And I'm not going to lie to myself by saying
I have all the facts that matter
My proofs are indefensible
Nothing you can say can make me believe
My words demand your respect
Because at the root is egocentric pride
Ignorance of grounded logic equals deniability
I love being right more than selfless
When did I ever claim to be principled?
When I listen to myself expounding, I must ask
Am I as wrong as my constituents say I am?

(now read bottom up)

Truth be Told

Bruce Lader

I am real,
and separate.

A mirror needs light,
I do not.

I will never abandon
my ungodly gift.

I defy the blissful fix
of worship, obey,
get into Heaven.

I choose
not to surrender my soul
as one might
remove clothing
before a shower,
or in the hour of prayer
kneel.

Typing Lesson

Carl 'Papa' Palmer

The quick brown fox jumps over the lazy dog

"All the letters in the alphabet are used," Mom explains as she checks the printed results for clarity, spacing and alignment on each typewriter in the office supply section of the Salvation Army Thrift Store before buying hers.

"It's called a pangram, however the word THE is used twice. This sentence can be shortened by replacing one of them with an A."

"*Pack my box with five dozen liquor jugs* is an even shorter pangram," she smiles, "however not something an upstanding church secretary like me would type."

When Cars Were America

Ed Ruzicka

Granny got a Caddie.
Got ahold of gold keys given
by her doctor son one Christmas.

She said, "Pile in my polliwog.
Pile in the back seat."
Let's fly off to Seven-Eleven
for Icees after pre-school.
Big air-puffed Coke, Strawberry Coke,
you suck down with a fat straw.
Gives you shivers in your throat back
in the deep comfort of my Cadillac.

Blue as the big blue sea,
Granny's Caddie whizzed along the fast lanes.
It had photosensitivity too,
a bitty-chip that shut the
lights down. Shut the lights down
when stubby-as-a-gremlin granny
didn't remember to do that thing.

How she grinned to tell her cousins
that the M. D. son gave his mum
her big blue Caddie Christmas.
Knew she knew they knew
she's the very one that made it.
Became the apple in the family pie.
Then went zoom-zoom on and on.

Tedious

Michael Estabrook

And so it begins
her step-sister married
a billionaire (with a "B")
and she's so
damned proud
of this guy's billions
that her stories
of extravagant consumerism begin
and she's not smart enough
to realize
how tedious it is
having to hear how the rich
spend their money.

Found on a Package of Frida Kahlo Socks

Jan Chronister

Caution!
(You may be arrested for the murder of Leon Trotsky.)
This product might be addicting due to
fashion sense, constant compliments ...
(traditional dress wins points in New York)
your loved ones stealing
(an affair with the heir of Fallingwater)
your socks
(will be useless after amputation),
friends wanting to borrow them.
It may also cause ...
an overwhelming sense of pride
(as the dove subdues the elephant,
your life a ribbon around a bomb).

After Sunrise, All Is White

R Scott Sexton

Raven
peers through frosted Paper Birch branches—
Studies the darkness.

She ruffs her feathers—clears her throat—

Rhyme Ice crackles, Shriek-squeaks in response.

Darkness deepens as Aurora whispers "listen".

Silent, soundless, surreptitious pad of lynx's paw.
Stammer of wind—
Convulsing Black Spruce shudder, shedding snow.

Black eye observing—contemplating—yellow eye, cogitating—
Feather ——— fur.

NO, Humility—Passivity—Pride—Hubris
here,
Not here among the rabbit pelt detritus.

Birthday in Bled

Felix Purat

Catching wind of the healing
Lake Bled bestows
I glance at my turquoise reflection
Deluded by tranquil waters

The next year begins and
Storm clouds descend with
Unchecked pride,
Proof of a future promising naught

Gazing from the high castle
There is little I have fought for:
In troubled Balkania, nothing is proven
If my holding a spear can't defend decaying walls

The rainstorm of pride intimidates the isle
Its little church knows no tranquility now
Nor will I if the walls aren't abandoned, for
Even on my birthday I am only a tourist.

Slovenia, 2017

The Fall

Howard Brown

Second best didn't sit well with Lucifer.
It was an affront to his vanity, a slight
which stung deeply and in anger he
gathered a host of like-minded angels
to do battle with God, a conflict he should
have known he would lose, even as the
idea first formed in his mind.

Of course, he suffered an epic, empyrean
ass-whipping (or so the story goes) and,
as with all things, there were consequences.
No longer known as *Son of the Morning Star*,
he was cast out of heaven, doomed to live
out the rest of eternity in hell, as *Satan, the
Prince of Darkness*.

So, if pride can bring an archangel low, ask
yourself what it might do to a mere mortal?

Shame, Shame

Ron. Lavalette

This was supposed to *be* something.
This was supposed to be worthwhile;
supposed to be something that
summed up and crowned his works,
glorified everything he'd done so far.

He wanted to be proud of his work;
wanted to be approached by readers,
wanted to see their heads still spinning,
their hands eager to shake his hand.
He wanted to hear them sing his praise.

No one even seemed to notice. No one
approached him for an autograph or
formed a line for a photo op. No one
betrayed the slightest interest. No one.

He gave up caring. He put down his pen.

Pride of Authorship

Jemshed Khan

You sink as you read a rival's writing:
so good you should quit, *now*

Like when your older brother
had you in headlock.

Or your lover's tongue
lacerated the honeyed wound.

The voice in your head says:
Oh, what's the use of even trying.

And you don't know
if you should even listen

to the voice of you
talking to you

as you reel
from the latest indignity

and your head lurches
like a top out of spin

and mostly want to curl up
inside your self

but instead you make a stand
out of a bruised eye

and bloody lip
because for now this is the fight

you're in.

The Simple Girl

Colleen Moyne

He loved a simple girl
born with neither beauty nor grace,
a face
that never turned a head

Though he came from wealth,
a privileged public life,
with a beautiful wife
confident and well-bred

Still he loved the simple girl,
kept away from public view
No-one knew
this secret kept for years.

She loved him too
but it was never more than this
He would not risk
the judgement of his peers

She did not have
the breeding they required
They would not understand
this girl below his station

And so he kept
his secret, simple girl
hidden from the world
to protect his reputation.

Annual Physical at 55

Karla Linn Merrifield

I scan my body for scars,
their degrees of visibility,
at middle age, visit long-familiar
ones two-score or more old:

Center right knee, a gray polka dot
above my patella, pretty well masked
when I'm tanned, in shorts. I fell
on my bike, skidded out, ground
cinders into skin, got up, got
my bearings, trod home, uphill
all the way— brave eight-year old.
Check. Right-o.

Laterally just below chin line
like a second faint smile;
can't detect it without a mirror
in good light, but my thumb reports
its ever-present line. At twelve, I fell
ice skating—no broken mandible,
no cracked tooth, no injured pride.
Still there, yes, still there.

And right upper arm, my most senior
cicatrix, shiny half-dollar like a spastic's
badge worn for fifty years. I fell
into a drunken doctor's hands;
they botched the shot too close
to the humerus bone, botched
the stitches—sewed a sad permanence.
I got it, no problem.

One, two, three.
All present.
At least these scars I can
account for, these scars I can see.

Even Steven

Anna Purves

We always tell each other when we've been lying
—no more than three months afterwards.
I've hated her mother for her
—just when she's needed me to,
and she's returned the favor
—sometimes with a little *too* much vigor.
We can always pick up right where we left off
—which is often intensely annoying.

She's never made friends with computers
which I tend to hold against her
—and I know she can tell.
I have to print out my emails to her,
then take them to the post office
and so I expect reimbursement for the stamps
—which she holds against me—
so you see, it all works out.

Most recently we darted off hither and yon
on separate trips with our separate spouses
and dang if we didn't bring each other back
an exotic sea shell, both of them a conch
like the kind you see Greek sea gods blowing on
in old-fashioned paintings

although mine, I have to admit, was smaller
—a lot smaller actually—
and one of the points was broken off
but mine was more legitimate and extraordinary,
having been found, by me, by the actual seashore
and hers, pinkly perfect,
was clearly purchased from one of those tourist-only shops.
Nonetheless, it was true synchronicity
the kind we've come to expect,
proof of the eternal alignment of our stars.

How many years we've dearly complained away the hours
—except that one time when I failed to understand
just what about my actions was so terribly unforgivable
so I insisted we'd have to agree to disagree—
Even so, we've shown up for every and all
of each other's events and occasions,
never needing to ask if we're coming.

But in these happy customs there has appeared
a bone in the ointment, a fly of contention
in the pattern of our tallied reciprocity
which is that I at least have realized
that the future will allow only one of us
at the other's funeral, and I,
who am so very fond of grudges
—and so proud how I've managed our symmetry—
am not one hundred per cent sure
which will be the worse end to be on.

The Drunken Cock

Chad Rohrbacher

Nature always sides with the hidden flaw,
and the Hungarian farmers
simplified it to the slow burn.
Rumor or myth, no matter,
they know a single dose of grain alcohol
will make the cocks assume
maternal behavior.

Now the chickens worry less
about their offspring
and the farmers realize the wealth
of stress-free poultry.
Scrambled, poached, over-easy or fried,
grandmothers on budgets bake more soufflés
while teenagers drive nails through shells,
work lips and tongue, drinking dreams
of muscles taught and supple,
muscles strong enough to embrace girls
under moonlight, in cars, in foldout pages,
yes, there are enough eggs to go around.

For the chicken it's all routine.
The egg, the cold fingers ruffling feathers, the day
of pecking dirt for grain and insect,
while the uninterested cock drinks, shot for shot,
calls out the sun and parades around the yard,
all while nudging chicks toward adulthood.
At least it has enough decency
to wait for the afternoon sun to warm the feathers
before clawing home drunk, so proud
of its chicks, overconfident of its contribution.

Pride

Cormac Stagg

It is a strange conundrum a mystery of decline, that I can see the pride twig in your eye, but can't see the log of pride in mine.

Now pride is the most fearsome sin because it dwells elusively, so deep down far within. Yes self-deception is pride's cunning plan, and it was always thus, since in Eden's garden, our hidden prideful time first began.

O Yes our antecedent mythic forebears made the first prideful play, you see. To be like God, or better yet, to make God be more like the all-important, egocentric, self-sufficient me.

And so it is our destiny to be poor subjects of our pride's incessant self-congratulatory toasts. Yes, it's always there with hyperbole and boasts, just like a grandiose, self-seeking, ego-driven ghost.

It is a strange conundrum a challenge to refine, that I can see the pride twig in your eye, but can't see the log of pride in mine.

Now pride is at its ruthless shameless best when it conceals its deep desire for power and bling. With pompous shows designed to hide its ostentatious and separating sting.

O yes pride proclaims with over confident absurdity, that all will be well, if you just follow me. For surely you desire to be a winner for the all the world to see? So come on now and swear your undying allegiance to the proud and perfect unassailable big me.

But pride has a dastardly and secret trump card in its oversized and brash war chest. For it will transform my deep desire for greatness into a sad and lonely quest.

It is a strange conundrum a riddle to define that I can see the pride twig in your eye, but can't see the log of pride in mine.

Now if I should decide when all's asunder, that this pride life is not for me, I must firstly fully concede that pride won't let me be. And even more importantly or so it seems to me, that of myself I don't possess the power to make pride flee.

For if I could it's plain enough for all to see, it would be just one more self-deceived expression, of pride still running rampant in the hidden life of me.

Yes powerlessness is the pure antidote to pride's relentless plea. The tried and tested cure of humility, if practiced, holds the essential key. To pride being once more banished, from the enchanted garden of pride-free liberty, that's waiting now to flourish deep down within the other centered, grace dependent, you and me.

It is a strange conundrum a mystery sublime, that when the log of pride is grace removed from my eyes, I don't see the twig of pride in thine.

From Invincible to Invisible

Mark Hudson

When I was in grade school, I took pride in creating my own Halloween costumes. One year, I took a big cardboard box, cut holes in it for the arms and eyes, painted it yellow and black and went as Swiss cheese.

Another year, I made myself a homemade pirate suit. I had a cardboard eye patch, and a plastic knife as part of my costume. When I got to school in second grade, a friend had a store-bought pirate costume, with a "real" eye patch, a Captain's hat, and a plastic cannonball attached to his leg. He had outdone me!

Not to be deterred, we were at a school parade, and we were to march around the field and show off our costumes. I still managed to walk around, proud of my home-made pirate costume, like the emperor with new clothes. Till I tripped and fell in a puddle, and everybody laughed.

Someone who heard this story said, "And that's where it all began."

I was no football player, or honors student, so growing up, I would do anything to get attention from my peers.

One day in jr. high, there was a park with a sign about ten feet high, with bushes right below them. Someone dared me to stand up on the sign, and do a belly flop into the bushes below. As I stood on top of the sign, the peer who dared me to jump off the sign said to passing peers, "You have to see this! Mark Hudson is going to do a belly-flop into the bushes!"

By now, a huge crowd had gathered around. There was no turning back. I gathered my courage, and leaped off the sign, doing a belly flop into the bushes. The bushes broke my fall, and I escaped uninjured.

Living in my hometown all
my life, I recently drove by that park
in a car with a friend, and the sign
was no longer there. For some
reason that made me feel old,
as if everything keeps changing
in my hometown, and I'm an
old man reminiscing.

I blamed my weirdness on my
family. I thought my family were the
biggest nerds in the area. One time,
my family were going to take us to
the local amusement park. I was
embarrassed to be seen with my
family, so I jumped out of
the car and ran back home. So
we didn't get to go that day,
just because of me.

Thankfully, though,
as I grew older and matured,
and realized that my family
cared for me, and nobody
in the real world would
ever care like they did, I
paid them back by showing
them love.

Until Mama's Proud of Me

Beatrice Preti

The sun's long gone, but my light still burns
Three books lay open; there's so much to learn
I cram it in my brain, but it only half-sticks
Repetition and revision spell the logical fix
I study around the clock, extra books on top of class
With only success in mind; there's no choice but to pass
Of all my waking moments, not a single one is free
I'll work and climb right to the top until Mama's proud of me
While the other kids are texting and sneaking out of school,
I also have my motives for subtly breaking rules
During P.E. I wear headphones, playing podcasts on repeat,
And I doodle physics equations on my graded homework sheets
I sneak out of the cafeteria to grab another pen
And I click off computer assignments to access Wikipedia again
During recess I don't gossip; I review my notes instead
My goals float in the clouds, so that's where I keep my head
I study twice, thrice as hard, harder than anyone I know
To test the fates and try my luck to see how far I'll go
Because when I reach the peak of life, that's when she'll finally see
That I can be a shining star, and I'll make Mama proud of me
We'll finally walk side-by-side down crowded city streets
She will brag about me to just about everyone she meets
I'll be someone and she'll be everything, just like life should be
It's the thought that will keep me going until Mama's proud of me

Those Eyes, Those Damned Eyes

William Butler

Hazel. They were hazel,
no, not brown, she told me,
looking directly into my face,
and it was the eyes, yes.
But that moment passed then,
both of us in other, separate worlds.
Watch the years roll by,
see us in remarkably similar
yet not, really,
circumstances.
But one night,
one quietly burning night,
there we were again,
flaring in a room crowded with wives and husbands.
Us
There were no other eyes there.
None.
I seized that fire,
offered those eyes, those hazel eyes,
love, lust, intense being-ness.
All.
Those eyes, those hazel eyes laughed.

Looking blatantly into my face,
she laughed, told me,
"You had your chance."
What was there to say?
Other men were there,
she clung to several
arm in arm, smiling up at them,
hazel eyes shining.
Watch several more years scroll along,
then,
one of those odd circumstances,
happenstance, serendipitous merging of comets
crashing, sparking, flaring.
And I felt my groin tighten,
blood rushing southward
while my heart thudded loudly.
We left together,
our hands busy in my car,
a suddenly dark evening
incandescent!
I held her away for a moment,
looked into her hazel eyes,
those smoky hazel eyes,
and asked about her husband.

The woman next to me

Chuka Susan Chesney

The woman next to me

is trying to photoshop
but she doesn't know how to photoshop
She doesn't know how to anything hop
I feel sublime as I know what to do
This is my job I'm a Florentine dream

P-17 she keyboards the screen
nothing appears but a blizzardy scene

The woman next to me receives way less attention
she gets befuddled by her fingertips
Someone comes by and tells her she's stuck
then asks me how my Simonetta will look
as an animated figure
in their Internet ad
She'll be Botticelli I reply as I should

The woman next to me goes to the ladies' room
gets lost in the hall when she's coming back
THIS ROOM IS FOR ARTISTS ONLY
NO VISITORS NEED APPLY
the spines of my voice whirl her round the inner glass

I puffer fish my Venus a few seconds later

An image has appeared with raspberry cheeks
Her face altarpieced on my Apple window
I infuse her with hues as I suck my Ovaltine

Tap tap again and my Archangel hovers

The woman next to me tea kettles over and over
P-17 she types on the screen
nothing happens
just an artless mist

The woman next to me is keyboarding snow
Poisoned by my pride
she's a washed-out road

The "self-made" man

Marsha Mittman

the "self-made" man so proud
of his many accomplishments
and truly justifiable because
he was an innovator and
major leader in his field

but nobody could tell him anything
he'd cut them off with a demeaning look
or a dismissive wave of his hand since
he considered himself an authority
even in fields he knew nothing about
and if perchance he didn't understand
a concept or a person he'd belittle
them as of no consequence

his pride ultimately alienating
his wife, children, and extended family
even workers who refused to
deal with his arrogance
and by never accepting anyone else's
credible input because he always
felt he knew better poor decisions were
inevitably made and his empire failed

leaving the "self-made" man in debt,
alone, and unloved, blaming everyone
and everything else for his fall from grace,
painfully clinging to his lost pride

An Acquired Taste —Or Not

Elizabeth Buttimer

How does pride taste when you swallow it?
I have found it to be like salt-water-taffy—
it seems to grow bigger, bigger and bigger
—with an eventual volume larger than the mouthful
that first went in. Then, it just won't slide
down the gullet. There's always one lumpy
place that won't let it go easily—won't let it pass
just when I think it's on a steep downhill grade
ready to totally gulp, it's like a runaway
eighteen-wheeler on an icy mountain pass
it slides—swerves—screeches—like the weight
shifts hard left—then, strains hard right—
then, shudders up a truck escape lane
to rest parallel to the through traffic
but not pass down that road to the right exit.

Worse yet, that taffy sticks to my teeth, grabs
my silver fillings and threatens a porcelain crown
the dentist put in last week.—No, I can't say
that I like the taste of pride when I swallow it.
Seems like I'm eating a fiery horseradish
sandwich, my tongue—a flame from nothing but
horseradish, bread and no water—and all that trouble
from having an opinion about myself, heaped up
so high—it's beyond the bounds of decency.

No, I've learned to try to leave pride alone,
altogether—but he's a sneaky rascal, just when
I slam the screen door in his face or shove-it-shut
on his foot wedged-in-the-gap between open
and closed, pride just slides on through
despite my effort at gate-keeping but I'll try
to close him out or keep him restrained
so I won't have to sup on that sorry so-and-so,
that jigger-full of undiluted vinegar, again.

His Rightful Place

Sara Abend-Sims

she was lovely once
now her nose is broken
her lip is often split
the kid is also not quite right

he thought of leaving
but didn't
and now he strikes her once
and once again
she shudders
palms hiding face

he strikes her third time round
then kicks and grabs the kid
she launches at him screaming
he drops the kid
reaching for the bottle

the following morn he is sober
last night a sprawling blank
they are sober too
with darkness in their eyes

this is my right, he thinks
last night's events alive now
my right, I am the man
the head, the iron-fisted ruler
he wallows in rightful pride
they are scum

at the funeral she doesn't speak
the kid reads a poem
he whispers at the end
'We won't miss you, dad'
the journo reports – 'We'll miss you'
in a tiny column his work requested
nobody bothers to correct

it was his right
he was the man the head
the iron-fisted ruler
she was a mouse, a scumbag
the one who sprinkled
Thal-rat into his bowl of soup.

Coming of Age

Gerard Sarnat

Early rainy Sunday morning we arrived at the sangha
for four hours of meditation then a closing dharma talk.

When someone's toe touched my slower heel
during mindful walking in our crowded hall
where people crept in every direction like bumper cars
toward end of an arcade ride after power's turned off,
I got triggered, looked up, mini-fumed at what turned out
to be an old friend who whispered, "Is that your grandson?"

"Yes!"

"He's the youngest person I've ever seen in my fifty years here.
Sits on his cushion tentpole straight like a veteran."

Just back from caring for endangered orphaned baby elephants
in Thailand, Simon assisted forest monks who also instructed
him as he dove into a fifteen minute twice a day practice
plus began to read Thich Nhat Hanh.

Driving home, my oldest grandchild shares how wonderful
it is to learn techniques to settle his head,
and I in turn share with him details
of a totally surprising twenty minutes alone
in Dharmsala's airport transit room
arranged by an Indian benefactor
with the Dalai Lama.

Today is a gift freely offered to both of us
in preparation for his bar mitzvah in three months.

I remind myself not to seem too proud.

Agamemnon Sets Sail from Troy, with Cassandra in Tow

Robert Cooperman

I should never have chosen the mad witch,
screaming, "Blood, everywhere." A slut as well,
for I assumed she'd plead to be left intact,
as when she duped the Archer, Apollo
that she'd trade her favors for the gift of Sight.
I looked forward to taking my pleasure
on her while she first begged me to desist,
then to ram into her and never stop.

Instead, the mad whore clawed my robes, costing
more than what she'd fetch in Asia's slave markets,
then she mounted me, great Agamemnon!
Worse, she shrieked, "You dirty, murdering Greek,
you'll be dead soon enough, and so will I."

No one believes a word the witch utters,
I least of all, loved by the Olympians
in my wealth and power, the king who's had
to sacrifice my dear oldest daughter:
the gods commanding her life for a fair wind
to the glory-striving plain of Ilium.

Still, her death haunts me, spearing me awake
to sob; Cassandra bathing me with a cloth,
then the soothings one might use on a child
and not the king who razed her golden Troy.
Then she lisps kisses against my forehead,
my mouth, then her talons flash and scratch me
as if, in her frothing, I'm the woman,
which more than her shrieking, "Blood everywhere"—

to panic my men stroking for Mycenae,
muttering I should toss her overboard—
fill me with a fright that she's desperate
to gorge on me before something dreadful
occurs, our thrashings ended forever.

Brave Pride

Albert DeGenova

We sold our house
to a black family.
In 1965, in Chicago, when the unwritten
rules were clear,
we broke the covenant.
My father on the run
from the bank, he had no more
buy-now-pay-later excuses.

I believed my father's swagger,
his explanations for sneering neighbors:
they were just jealous
of his new TV and his
big car, my mother's fur coat.
His bought-into dreams
discolored and deferred.

Another father
scraping a path out of
housing projects just two blocks away
claimed his piece of a used and tarnished dream –
a simple brick bungalow on a 25-foot lot.

This brave black family chose
to live among Poles Italians Irish—
on one side a family so arrogant they refused to speak—
on the other side, a clan of eight kids, including a boy
who ate dirt with a tablespoon in the front yard,
their house so close you could join in their breakfast conversation—
and next to them
new-world fascists who sent their son out to play
dressed in military uniforms.

Green was the only color
my father saw in front of him,
a family with a proud
down payment clenched
in a strong working man's hand.

Broken, we moved
into a two-bedroom basement apartment
heads down on a rainy October afternoon.

The Changing of the Guards Cometh After a Fall

Ken Gosse

"Veni, vidi, vici."
Our proudest confession
as nation by nation
became our possession;
an onslaught with no need
for slightest digression
until we encountered
the people called Hessian—
stupendous in spirit and brawn.

While showing, as always,
the noblest expression,
we'd lord over fools
whose pathetic obsession
was focused on thwarting
our gentle aggression—
of which we relented
to their repossession,
for Lo! They would have us all gone.

"Run Away! Run Away!"
Oft' the wisest concession.
The bravest all know
that there is no transgression
to temper one's valor
with all due discretion
and recede, not proceed
("Strategic Regression"),
when fate says it's time to move on.

And now, as we march home
in royal procession,
fair damsels still swoon
at our roguish impression:
brave knights in bright armor—
the Finest Profession.
But e'er we return,
we take time to refreshen
the armor we soiled at dawn.

Parental Echoes

Shane Guthrie

I was depressed
I looked out at a pretty day and thought:
"why bother. the gray is inside me, it goes with me"

Help was a call away
But I never thought of calling
You taught me strength
By teaching me not to ask

I can walk on a broken leg a long time
I can walk on it for years
Never tending it, wincing
        Shameful tears come to my eyes
              But I stay silent

Breaking was not the problem
It was that destroying pride you gave me
That kept me broken

I wanted to apologize
But my tongue was covered in my dad's words
Of 'shut up' and 'get up' and 'do it now'

I knew it was wrong
My belly filled with frogs
My head buzzed hot with wasps

I want to call it pride
Bruised purple and standing angrily
My experience and my cleverness
I was right

But it was shame at being unable
To articulate, to convince, to prove
And to refuse to understand, to listen
I'd become that same stubborn asshole
That, right or wrong, was insufferable

Trying to cover my mistakes with my glories
Like wrapping my shit in silk
No one is fooled

Bathroom Reading

Emery Veilleux

Unlock iPhone
Open: Safari
Open: New Tab
pain after peeing
blood after peeing
is blood after peeing a symptom of a UTI
UTI symptoms
Open: New Tab
natural home remedies for UTI
can cranberry juice cure a UTI
how much sugar is in cranberry juice
does sugar make you bloated
how bad for you is cranberry juice
does sugar make it hard to sleep
blue light effects on sleep
Lock iPhone
Unlock iPhone
Open: New Tab
UTI isn't going away
have they disproven cranberry juice
how to get antibiotics
how much do antibiotics cost
how much does a pharmacist make
does insurance cover emergency room

how long can I stay on my parents' insurance
hospitals near me
Open: New Tab
can you take too many probiotics
how does yogurt work
best kinds of yogurt for probiotics
jamie lee curtis age
Open: New Tab
vulva swollen and itchy
antibiotic side effects
antibiotic side effects yeast infection
how do you know if you have a yeast infection
Open: New Tab
cottage cheese consistency
cottage cheese images
cottage cheese recipes
are yeast infections viral
can men get yeast infections
what is yeast
how much does monistat cost
natural home remedies for yeast infection
Close: Safari
Lock iPhone
Unlock iPhone
Open: Safari
Open: New Tab
small syringe price
will greek yogurt stain my underwear
garlic in vagina debunked?
Open: New Tab
UTI not going away

early signs of cervical cancer
is cervical cancer fatal
how long do you have to live if you have cervical cancer
how much does chemo cost
natural home treatments for cervical cancer
best foods to kill cancer
why is turmeric so gross
why is life so hard
Open: New Tab
does dying hurt
first signs of active dying
how to induce a natural death
am I suicidal
are a lot of people suicidal
do men make women suicidal
what is the afterlife like
which religion has the best afterlife
reaching nirvana in six months
how do you know if you're going to hell
priests near me
Open: New Tab
how to say goodbye to your family when you are dying
how much does grief counseling cost
do I need a will if I don't own anything
can I wear jewelry when I'm cremated
urns that aren't ugly
how much does a mortician make
will mortician shave my head
will mortician shave my body
will mortician shave my vagina
is necrophilia illegal

can you go to hell after you're already dead
can dead body still have a yeast infection
Open: New Tab
how long does it take for antibiotics to work
Clear Search History
Close Safari
Lock iPhone

Prose

75	Widow's Pique	*Jan McCarthy*
79	Then go	*Duncan Strachan*
80	Turd Burglar	*Steve Cushman*
82	The Astronomy of Childhood	*Len Kuntz*
84	Bombay Calling	*Eddy Knight*
88	Being a Man	*RubinA*
89	Before a Fall	*Sue Dawes*
91	Frontline Symphony	*Henry Bladon*
93	Devil's Drop	*Mark Crimmins*
97	The Beard	*Joseph Stearman*
99	Crimson	*Cynthia Leslie-Bole*
101	On Quitting Your Job and Looking Back	*Peter Michal*
105	The Root of All Evil	*Paul Beckman*
107	Chef's Surprise	*Jim Bell*
111	Predators	*Mary Krakow*
113	Heavy Petal	*Peter Lingard*
117	Exercising Retribution	*Jo Hocking*
121	Finding Mailman Dante	*Ruth Z. Deming*
124	The Recent History of the Sánchez Family Tragedies: Part VII	*Guilie Castillo Oriard*
128	Self-Exposure	*Charles David Taylor*
132	The Pink Hotline	*Tom Fegan*

134	The Return of Red Ledbetter Episode 7	*JP Lundstrom*
139	The Blue Ribbon	*Steve Carr*
143	Victoria Seizes the Reins	*Larry Lefkowitz*
147	Woodhouse Moor	*Nod Ghosh*
152	My Final Testament	*Chris Hall*
154	Balancing Cheques	*Pat O'Connor*
157	The Parable of the Bread	*Lia Lewis*
159	Hospice	*Norman Klein*
163	The Beauty of a Vacation	*Annabelle Baptista*
166	The Tyrant's Garden	*Aaron Retz*

Widow's Pique

Jan McCarthy

I should never have got involved in their stupid competition. You'd think at my age I'd have a million strategies for repelling boarders, but I let myself get sucked. What a prize idiot! It's costing an arm and a leg. I'm already having to cut corners in the weekly food shopping, but what can I do? Can't back out. *I never back out.* Call it stubbornness, call it pride, call it whatever you like. Born that way. But I'm getting ahead of myself.

What started it was, I had to move house. Nearly broke my heart, moving from the four-bed where Gerard and I brought up our kids to this tiny bungalow miles from town. Back to back with another one the same. Ten-by-twelve front garden in a line of ten identical little boxes. Same opposite. Net curtains a priority. No room indoors to swing a cat. Humiliating, to be honest, but I didn't fancy an apartment and can't manage stairs, so it was my only option.

The kids and grand-kids are scattered to the four winds. *Got to go where there's work and a proper future, Mum,* but Singapore? Osaka? New bloody *Zealand?* Really? I reckon they just abandoned ship before I got incontinence, or dementia, or both.

Eldest son Harry moved me in just before he, skinny Clarissa and the brood disappeared off to Auckland. To be fair, they did stick around to make sure my single, solitary wardrobe and orthopaedic arm-chair were in the right places, and Clarissa got the curtains hung up. Can't stand people gazing in. But they didn't take me out to tea as promised. Maisie was blubbing in the back of the car, thirteen and emotionally unhinged, so they cut it short. I let them go and didn't cry. I have my self-respect. I put the kettle on, opened a packet of biscuits and got on with it.

Next-door neighbour turns up at eight-thirty the following morning with a plate of cookies and a business-like air about her. *I'm Shirley from number six*, she says, sticking her hand out, *welcome to the neighbourhood.* I couldn't very well leave her standing there so I let her into my teeny-tiny kitchenette and made a brew. *You'll be wanting to crack on with your front garden*, says she of the purple rinse, nibbling on her biscuit and giving me a no-nonsense look, *the last one let it go. Died in here as a matter of fact.*

By the time she'd drunk three cups of tea, scoffed half the cookies and rattled on like an old cattle wagon, it was getting on for lunch-time. No way was I going to share my ham sandwiches, so I told her I had things to do and got rid. Drew the front curtains, sat down in my arm-chair and put the radio on Classic FM to calm me down. I was seeing those weird goldy-swirly triangles in front of my eyes that mean a migraine's coming on. Time I'd taken forty winks it was five, so I took a cool shower and took the ham sandwiches to bed with me. Thought I'd drop off again real quick, but at midnight, there's me, lying awake staring at the ceiling, already full of ideas.

Seems the street's won a neighbourhood front gardens award for the past twenty-five years, and the rest of 'em are ganged up to make sure I don't go letting the side down. There's prize money, group photo in the paper, barbie at Shirley's if you get the gold. There was a veiled threat in the way she said it, like *Don't expect anyone to call the paramedics if you drop of a heart attack in the street if you don't join in.* Something kinda scary in her eyes. Not what you'd expect. I mean, old people are supposed to be more mellow.

Clarissa'd been about to dump Gerard's gardening books in the box for the opshop, but luckily I'd stopped her in time. Gerard's notes in the margins, lovely handwriting. I went and rummaged around till I found them, took a coffee and some of Clarissa's carrot cake back to bed, along with a notebook and pen, and started planning a front garden that'll knock the others into a cocked hat.

You can't go planting just anything. Bad for the environment. Got to think of the grand-kids, poor buggers. Line of prickly tea-trees along the front, feature stone fountain in the middle, encircled by ruby saltbush for colour. Most of the neighbours have stuck to gold and green, but I was thinking of the old flag. There's a cash prize for the best front garden. I'll show that Shirley who she's dealing with! Blue's easy: everyone loves the native bluebell. Add some running postman in pots and a sweet apple-berry against the side fence, and Bob's your uncle.

Next morning, feeling a bit worse for wear but excited, I caught the minibus that takes us wrinklies to town and back three times a week, and spent a small fortune at the garden centre. The nice man saw all my stuff – the plants and the four bags of white gravel – and offered me a lift home. Nice man. My age, at a guess, nicely turned out the way Gerard always was, until they took him into the hospice. *Brendan*, he said, *happy to help*. Gave me his phone number when he dropped me off, and stayed for a quick chat. Even offered to come over and help with the garden, but I'll have to have a think about that. I don't want any romantic entanglements. I got one of his junior staff in to install the fountain.

Well, better crack on. Shirley's sat on a stool outside her place, peeling spuds. Good moment to get the running postmen potted up and start pouring gravel. Painkillers: check. Gardening hat: check. Grim and determined smile: check. I'm not about to let anyone see I wish I'd never started.

Then go

Duncan Strachan

Write a line, then go and go and go and go and what comes to mind? Let those who live bury their dead, and those who are dead go free, but while I live, I shall live and be happy. What a bastardised thought. Note to self: never try to remember word for word the blurb to another Tolstoy epic. How is it that memory can fail so promptly? It's like standing in front of a curtain, the memory being projected behind it, and all you have to watch the memory is a mirror that you look into and that reflects what's happening behind the curtain—think David Lynch's red curtained room. And where might he be at the moment? Golly, I feel like a TMZ editor, is this how they think, only in the geographical and general aesthetic of celebrities? Why be so cynical. They are no doubt people with hopes, with dreams, with families who hassle them or don't hassle them, with thoughts despairing and nuanced. I mean, I started out with a line about what comes to mind, and then began thinking about the geographical vicinity of film maker and celebrity David Lynch, I mean, that's a point of empathy if anything. I'm like them. They could perhaps be like me?

Turd Burglar

Steve Cushman

Val and I were at the back window of our apartment. I was surprised when she let me walk up behind her and hug her as she looked out into the frosty December morning. Our backyard was littered with a half-dozen frozen piles of dog poop I hadn't yet got around to cleaning up.

"What's your plans for the weekend?" she asked.

"Don't know. I might go into work for a few hours." As soon as I said it I remembered that's what I'd told her on those nights when I hadn't actually gone to work.

"We could go get breakfast," I said.

"I'm not hungry."

"We could go shopping, maybe shoe shopping."

She loved shoes; I hated shopping.

"Maybe," she said.

She seemed about to turn away and leave when the three crows landed in the backyard and started their cocky march out by the birdbath. One of the crows headed for a pile of dog poop, which was frozen solid as a stick. He bit the poop-stick and flew away with it in his mouth hanging there like an un-lit cigar.

Val started laughing. "Did you see that?"

"I thought crows were supposed to be smart."

She shook her head. Her dark hair in my face, my eyes, my mouth. "Things ain't always what they seem."

She seemed content to leave that comment between us for a moment or two. And I held on to her because for the first time in what seemed forever she didn't push me away.

When the second crow walked to the same frozen poop pile and grabbed a small chunk and flew away, I said, "Turd burglars." For some reason this made her laugh, and for a few minutes we were a young couple in love again, discovering together all the mysteries of the world.

"Turd burglars," she said again and turned around and hugged me. She looked me in the eyes. Her eyes were misty, beautiful, something beyond what I deserved. I knew this was it, the moment she'd decide what was next for us. It wasn't up to me. I'd made my mistakes, begged for forgiveness. There was nothing else I could do. She kissed me twice on the forehead. When I tried to kiss her on the lips, she turned back to the yard, but she squeezed my hand against her belly.

One last crow sauntered over to that same pile of frozen poop. He seemed to consider it for a moment like his brothers before him and with pride tilted his head toward the sky and let out three strong calls. And then he flew up and away, leaving all that mess behind.

The Astronomy of Childhood

Len Kuntz

You are busy counting Saturn's moons, all sixty-two of them. One of your eyes is bigger than the other, and it's the smallest one that keeps all the secrets.

Mother left a note that no one's seen but you. Perhaps that's why you bray into the telescope, your bourbon breath fogging the lens.

Tonight, the stars weep while Luna wrings her hands. The sky smells like cigar smoke or the bottom of a burial urn. If you notice, you're not telling.

Inside the house, every framed photo is missing a person, or perhaps a missing person. It's hard to know which. Life is so difficult to order. There's too much porcelain and gold.

Still, the maid comes thrice weekly. Lately her lips dance and she smells like a garden of lavender. If I ask a question, her face gets stuck in traffic. I watch her polish and fondle our family crest that hangs above the mantel. Occasionally her lips kiss the shoulder of the capital letter while her tongue drags lower, wiping a shield.

The bedroom where you made us sometimes talks in its sleep, rewinding rumors, taking dumb luck for granted. Even the walls don't know what to think.

Your stay-pressed slacks and French cuff shirts hang like rows of scarecrows in the closet where Sis hides out while spinning more treasure. Me, I spend all day doing the math of living, honoring each equation the way you do astronomy and the distended spoils of your present future.

Bombay Calling

Eddy Knight

There's a tune that's been haunting me. Because of the phone calls.

You know them. The ones where there is no one on the other end, perhaps some faint electrical noises, occasionally a bit of far-off laughter, as if there is a party going on in a cave somewhere and you are not invited. You stand there saying "Hello…hello…hello," in case it is one of the grandchildren trying to tell you that "Mummy's fallen over and she's not moving." Just as you are reaching for the car keys an Asian voice comes on saying, "Hello, is that Mr. Martin? My name is Gracie and I am calling you from the Microsoft Technical Division about a problem with your computer."

I may be retired but I still have all my faculties about me and I am nobody's fool. I listen to a lot of music but I am also an avid Radio National fan and am well aware of the burgeoning scamming industry. So the first time I was called I just replied, "I'm afraid you must have the wrong number. I don't own a computer," and hung up. I lied of course, but so had she, and I saw no reason, then, to be impolite.

Rudeness generally upsets me. When I witness ill-mannered behaviour I pity the person who so demeans themselves. I'm not some tedious old pedant who believes we are being swept towards the apocalypse by a deluge of loutish behaviour. Most people are perfectly reasonable. I find the majority of shop-assistants helpful and often pleasantly amusing. I do not expect young people to give up their bus seat for me just because I have white hair. But for a very pregnant woman, or a frail old lady burdened down with shopping bags, I do feel that school-children should disengage themselves from their phones, just for a second, and stand. When they don't I just think, "Your day will come."

I still believe in the laws of karma. I was a hippy fifty years ago, before I became an academic. You wouldn't know it to see me in the street. I don't have a long plait hanging down behind a receding hair line. Or dreads, God help us. I haven't 'inhaled' for over a decade but I still listen to a lot of music. And not just the old stuff. It might be the Grateful Dead or Pink Floyd one minute but just as easily could be Elbow or Julia Holter. The sort of music shelved under 'alternative' in JB HiFi. I'm also partial to a bit of Debussy, some Erik Satie, even, occasionally, Shostakovich.

One obscure favourite from years ago was a band called It's A Beautiful Day, whose electric violin wailed like Coltrane's sax. They had this great instrumental track called *Bombay Calling*. I haven't heard it for years, but the phone calls reminded me.

You see they didn't stop. Every day the ringing intrudes upon my listening pleasure, disturbs my equilibrium. The voice isn't always Indian, sometimes it's Chinese, or other East Asian accent. They could all come from the same polyglot call-centre in Sydney, but I don't think so. The hiatus before they speak indicates overseas origins. Mostly they are Indian though, so that when my wife, as concerned as I about the welfare of family members, shouts in from the garden "Who was that, dear?" I now answer "Just Bombay Calling, love."

I registered with a national list that was supposed to prevent cold calling. It worked for a while, cutting off fundraising requests from registered charities, but I hadn't minded them. It was still mildly annoying but when it turned out to be for a worthy cause like epilepsy or animal welfare I had quite often donated.

Unfortunately the number of blatant rip-off calls seemed unaffected, indeed increasing in number, driving me wild. What particularly infuriates me is the casual assumption that I would fall for such brazen subterfuge.

As soon as I hear those empty seconds, the impulse to slam down the receiver rises in my gorge with such overwhelming pressure that the hand clutching the receiver starts to shake and my knuckles turn white.

Our daughter has two children under the age of five. So I maintain control, at no small cost, until the spiel kicks in. And sometimes it doesn't, just leaves me tottering on a nightmare's edge until someone at the far end of a malicious universe decides that they have tortured me enough, and rings off.

Finally I had had enough. I swore that, restrained as I had been so far for the sake of decorum, the very next caller was going to get both barrels, figuratively speaking.

So when Cheryl began her introduction I cut her off and jumped straight in with "Are you proud of the work you're doing?"

She sounded shocked. "Mr. Martin, pride is a sin."

That threw me. "Are you a Catholic?" I'd imagined a Moslem or a Hindu, maybe a Sikh. I was intrigued.

"Certainly Mr. Martin. Originally I came from Goa, where there are many Catholic families. According to Saint Augustine pride is the…"

"Commencement of all sin," I broke in and completed her quote. "I am a Doctor, not a Mister. I used to lecture on comparative religions."

"I am so sorry, *Doctor* Martin. I am a student myself, which is why I am doing this phone-call work. University here in India is very expensive."

"But surely there is other work."

"I am not pretty enough to sell myself, nor malformed enough to beg. All that I have is my voice and the power of speech."

That put me in my place. I felt compelled to listen. We talked for over an hour. She spun me her tale and my anger was gone. I even sent her a cheque, although I didn't tell my wife. Occasionally now she rings me up for a chat. The other calls didn't stop, but they did diminish in number.

Being a Man

RubinA

"But when?" she questioned me in her innocent voice. Her eyes were quizzing me, rather piercing through mine to know the truth behind the decision, the announcement I had just dared to make, 'that we will not meet again unless the destiny chooses to' and that we shall wait for the day and not run after it.

I simply loved the way, and at times was intrigued at the way, she understood the logic, the reasons behind my rash and unjust decisions, even when there were none mostly. I think that was my own way of troubling her for my indecision and all the impulsive flaws I wanted to hide in the garb of that commanding space she had positioned me. I would just always announce and she ... She would simply obey. How I was always scared of her submission and tried not to hate and belittle myself for acting so mean. I knew she would cry for days, months until I change my mind again and accept her as my best option. But her loyalty, her fidelity scared the hell out of me. The human in me wanted to love her, stay betrothed, give her the respect and honesty she deserves. I wanted to be yelled at, to be threatened, to be subjected to insecurity.

But the Man in me wanted to be wild and experimental. I can't really be a human if I am only a Man and realised how I was, for a second not so proud of being a Man.

Before a Fall

Sue Dawes

The voice cuts through the chapel ruins. I shiver, glance down at Boris who is circling the moss-filled roots of the twisted oak tree. His wet nose agitates the undergrowth. He is oblivious to everything except the scent of other dogs.

Help me.

I swallow, look around but there's no one else here. Is Hayley right? Is my mind starting to test me? But my daughter is unpredictable, one minute talking about moving in, the next fanning out nursing home brochures on my walnut coffee table.

I turn off my hearing aid because sometimes static sounds like sentences.

But the voice is still there, relentless in its plea. It corkscrews into my ear, the words pouring through.

Help me, help me, help me.

'Boris,' I call out, a tremor in my voice.

Boris answers by pushing through my legs and darting around the tree for the third time. Stumbling, I put my hand on the trunk for support. It burns and I snatch it away. Panicking I call 'Boris' again.

This is no time to have another heart attack.

I should have listened to Hayley and stayed closer to home.

Straightening up, I feel every bone in my spine snapping to attention.

I will not give in to old age

Now Boris is back by my side, his tail between his legs and someone's laughing, the maniacal sound leaks through the vegetation. I form my hands into awkward fists.

Then Boris licks my ankle and breaks the atmosphere, which hangs dense like the canopy of leaves above. The trunk is cool when I reach out again and it's then I notice the weeping legions slashed in the bark, as if something has been released from deep inside.

I stand up straighter.

I'm not ready to move or give up Boris but maybe a companion would be a compromise.

I'll tell Hayley tonight.

Frontline Symphony

Henry Bladon

My last day here. The familiar thumping of the rotors precedes the rush of the engines. The throb vibrates my eardrums. The Chinook makes an unmistakable noise – a boom that carries on the boiling air – announcing the arrival of the latest casualties way in advance. When I first arrived at this dusty hellhole, the sounds hit me and assaulted my senses. Over time, you become habituated.

The crashing of the doors is our cue; the screams of wounded soldiers have a haunting quality. A roadside bomb has blasted another vehicle on a routine mission. Even through my mask I can smell dust and sun and the acrid taste of explosives mingled with burnt tissue. The left leg is mashed: red and white images of bone and arterial blood cause me more concern.

'Okay, let's get to work.'

The insistent beeping from the monitor conveys anxiety, exhorting our efforts.

'The leg has to go.' Not a decision I take lightly, but it might save him.

Next follows the sound of saw on bone. Buzzing, grinding. The effervescent note of the blade rises and falls as I cut. It's both energetic and sad. He's losing part of himself to save the rest.

When I'm done the nurse moves in and I hear the fizz as

she seals the vessels. Then there's the satisfaction in the snap of latex. The sound of surgical gloves being removed does not always signify success, but today it is the sound of pride in a job well done and another early loss averted.

When the young soldier recovers enough strength, we'll fly him back home to recuperate. Minus his left leg, of course.

The following week, he's out of intensive care and I see him in the infirmary. I tell him he is my last ever casualty out here. He says he's honoured. His voice has the musical quality of gratitude. It's nice to hear, but of all the sounds I encountered, I'll never escape the echo of those screams.

Devil's Drop

Mark Crimmins

I'm on my red Ricochet and Jay's on his white Cannondale for our Sunday mountain bike ride. It's early and nobody's on the Squaw Peak Trail. On the way up, we pause at Devil's Drop. Jay explains the scary physics. The added momentum from the trail's sudden dip. The unexpected G force of the parabolic curve. The counterintuitive sharpness of the final switchback. He points to the cottonwood tree.

"Even visually, this tree prevents your mind from computing the danger. Until it's too late. But the real danger is behind the tree."

Straddling our crossbars, we shuffle forward to look at the long drop-off hidden by the tree's lower branches. The seventy-degree walls of Slate Canyon. A three-hundred-percent gradient. What the skiers called a Double Black Diamond. Jagged tiles of rock have flaked off the cliffs and fan into an accumulation hundreds of feet below.

This is all good to know. But at the same time, Jay's warnings annoy me. I pride myself on my downhill skills. Nobody descends like I do. Everybody knows that. I have super-quick reflexes and—one of my secrets—I have no fear. Negotiating the perils of Devil's Drop is well within my powers.

It's a tough ride to the top and takes two hours. Five thousand vertical feet, starting at six thousand. Up there, the views of the Wasatch Range are amazing. But I'm anticipating the descent. I've seen it time and again in the mountain bike races—no one can touch me on the downhill.

When we set off, I'm in the lead. Cautious Jay hangs back. I seem to be pulled down the mountainside much more quickly. It's like gravity is reeling me in. *Gravity is my friend*—that's my motto. My friends sometimes say my fearless downhill rides actually mask a death wish. But they're wrong. It's just me—the daredevil of descent. Nobody can stay with me, and I like it that way. Before long, I'm hundreds of yards ahead of Jay. Too far to hear his shouted warnings. Exhilarated by the downward rush, I plunge toward Devil's Drop along the vertiginous switchbacks of the narrow canyon trail.

By the time I remember Jay's admonitions I'm heading straight for the precipice. I brake, but it's too late. The bike leaves the trail and shoots into the branches of the cottonwood tree. I hear the clatter and rattle of snapping twigs and swishing leaves. The bike gets caught in the tangled branches. But I myself am airborne. Arms like outstretched wings, I sail out from the cliff ledge like a huge, heavy bird. I look down into the yawning chasm of space below me. The only good thing is that I'm flying in an elongated position. Like Superman. Head first, arms up ahead of me. This provides a fleeting illusion that I can steer myself. Navigate the thin canyon air. I take a deep breath—my last, perhaps—as I hurtle through the terrifying drop towards the rock face falling steeply away from me. My yells echo from the cliffs of the opposite canyon walls.

Time seems to slow down. I have time to register a few thoughts. The cliff face I'm about to hit is flaky. The shale is loose. My body is falling in the best possible orientation. I grimace and yell in preparation for landing. Hear the *whoooooaaaa!* and *aaarrrrrrggghhhhh!* of impact. Some kind of pop in my ears. All goes dark.

I'm temporarily blinded by a faceful of gravel and dust and

dirt. But the soft, loose slate absorbs a lot of my impact. It also facilitates my movement down the steep slope. Incredibly, I skid down the cliff wall on my belly. Thousands of tiny pieces of rock move under me. An avalanche of loose shale moves down the cliff with me. Pebbles rattle off my wraparound shades like hailstones bouncing of a windshield.

Finally, I come to rest by the creek at the bottom of the canyon. Stunned, I get to my feet and inspect my limbs one by one. Waggle legs, arms. Shake my head and neck. No broken bones! I raise my arms and let out a triumphant death-defying whoop. My voice sounds a bit weird. I dust myself off. Clear sand from my eyes, nose, mouth, throat. I have scores of little cuts and scratches on my arms and legs. But no severed arteries. No punctured organs. I feel my teeth. All there!

I look up at the cliff over which I have just plunged. Hundreds of feet above me I spot the red bike cradled in the cottonwood's branches. I've scored a deep groove down the mountain where I've ploughed into the shale like a crashing plane. Seeing this, I take deep breaths and shudder with temporary shock.

I look around for a route back up to the bike. I find one a few hundred yards down the canyon and clamber up to the trail. Finally, I walk around a bend and see the bike hanging in the tree. Jay is sitting slumped on a rock, head in hands, sobbing. I ask him what he's doing. My voice is weirdly muffled. I realize I've damaged my ears. He jumps. Eyes wide, he turns a shocked white face towards me. For a second, covered in dust, I look like my own ghost. Jay's surprise quickly turns to anger. He shouts loud enough that I can hear him clearly.

"Uh, I'm sitting here crying because I thought you were dead, asshole! Thanks for shouting up to let me know you were okay! I saw the skid marks. The bike in the tree." He brushes his tears into a dirty smudge across his face. "I kept calling down but there was no answer. Where the hell have you been?" He stands up.

I walk over, slap him on the back, and, putting my arm around his shoulder, answer with my strangely muffled voice.

"To hell and back, Dude—to hell and back!"

The Beard

Joseph Stearman

"You should shave your beard," she said.

He blushed, face red except for the parts covered by that brown, Viking-like bush. "Why?"

"Because, baby," she gathered her books, about to head out to her comm class, "you'll look more professional. It'll help you get a good job. And it feels scratchy when we kiss."

"Think I'll keep the beard," he said. He kept his eyes on the TV, into the basketball video game he loved so much.

"Mmm 'kay," she said. She kissed his head, then walked out the door. She'd been spending the night quite often, leaving bits and pieces of jewelry and makeup around his room.

He paused the game once the door closed, staring at the ceiling. He liked her. She was the first girlfriend he ever had. She cared for his future. She wanted him to get a good job, make good money. She wanted this for him. Right?

His beard was his pride. His father had one. His older brothers grew beards. His identity had become "The Beard" – even some professors called him by the nickname.

Except her. She called him John. And this was the fifth time in their three months that she mentioned shaving the beard. He was older now. A senior. It was about that time, wasn't it?

And so, when he looked in the mirror, holding the razor with white cream around the edges, he analyzed the stranger who gazed back. A clean slate. Younger. Sterile.

He felt ashamed.

She returned after class, halting in front of the open bathroom. An enormous grin spread across her pretty face. She hugged him tight. She kissed his soft cheek. "It looks so good, John."

She breezed into his bedroom. He held a hand where she kissed – where the dry lips left a sharp sting on his sensitive skin.

She called from the bedroom, "Now it's time to buy a suit!"

Crimson

Cynthia Leslie-Bole

A crimson bra, the color of hot blood, passion and seduction. Lace through which wanton flesh could flash. Clara fingered the lingerie on its hanger and wondered why she would never own such a thing, why she would never even dare to try it on, why she had to glance over her shoulder to make sure no one was looking as she touched the contoured push-up cups.

Clara imagined the kind of woman who would wear a red brassiere. She saw the woman strutting across her boudoir in stilettos, flaunting a garter and matching panties that cleaved her ass in two. A man sat back in an upholstered chair watching her while languidly smoking a cigarette. She twirled, arched her back, and put one shoe on the bed to adjust the strap unnecessarily so he could get a different view of her perfect derriere.

Clara felt herself congeal at the image in her mind and tried to banish it. But still she stood by the bra rack. The words *prideful, cheap,* and *slutty* floated through her mind in her mother's voice, but still she didn't walk away. In fact, she picked the bra off the rack and took a tentative step toward the dressing room.

"Can I help you find your size, Ma'am?" Hearing the saleswoman's voice from behind her, Clara blushed a matching shade but nodded and held out the bra mutely.

"Let's measure you then. You're a big-breasted woman, sweetie—might as well show off what you've got."

"No, no, it's not that," Clara squeaked. "I just want to try it on. Just to see." But the sales clerk had already left to retrieve her size.

Clara stood in the aisle feeling naked even though she was wrapped in her winter coat. But when the woman returned, Clara took the bra and stepped into the changing room.

"Would you like me to come in to help with the straps?"

"No, no, I'm fine, really."

Clara stared at herself in the mirror. Her breasts bulged out of the top of the bra, and her cleavage looked like the San Andreas fault. The color was a neon sign. The thing was ridiculous, inappropriate, tacky. Clara took the red bra off, slowly putting on her own stretched-out, greying bra. It was functional, no-nonsense and over-the-hill, just as she was.

Clara walked out of the dressing room. Without looking at the eager face of the saleswoman, she put the bra on the counter and uttered words that made her shake: "I'll take it."

On Quitting Your Job and Looking Back

Peter Michal

I have a group of friends. They're thirty-something, university-educated, professional people. They're in serious relationships. Some have children. They've all managed to buy, against the odds, a three-bedroom house with a backyard. They're also depressed and desperate. They blame work.

It's a funny stage of life.

No one is old enough for a mid-life crisis here. None of us wants to run off with the secretary; none of us have a secretary. We have a computer, a phone and a coffee mug, and only the mug belongs to us. If people have personal problems — relationships breaking down, family illnesses, addictions of any kind — then they don't talk about them. The problem is work. We talk about that. That's all we talk about.

If it could be weighted, only thirty per cent of the collective complaint would be about the work itself — seventy per cent would be about the people.

You can't do much about the former. It is what it is. You either learn to deal with the repetition and the lack of surprise in your life or you don't. The people and how they cooperate and treat one another, we should be able to change.

The complaints are varied but they have common threads: control and respect. These are universal themes, linking political power plays in the halls of Parliament to disputes about the coffee machine in <u>your</u> office.

In my office, there are four layers of management between daylight and me, and at every level ideas are killed off, control is enforced, the benefit of the doubt is not given, respect is not shown. The managers don't work together, they work independently. Each tries to show his or her worth by scrubbing out what the one below did. What survives this review process, what is left of that report you wrote, the idea you had, is what four people in separate rooms and at different times unconsciously agreed upon.

The way my friends see it, they create and drive innovation and technical change, and others critique. Everyone thinks their job is the most important job. Everyone thinks the place would fall apart without them.

You know it's time to go when you catch yourself in this thought.

An email was sent out the other day, another staff departure: *Since joining four years ago, Janine has tirelessly coded course materials to statistical classifications to support our data collections, contributing to the introduction of a new classification management system. Janine opted for a quiet exit; she left yesterday.*

Four years of your working life reduced to one sentence. This is every office worker's fate. Wondering what your own sentence will say is a depressing exercise.

Peter tried his best at first but then became disaffected and spent his last years with the company having complaints made about him for his tone of voice.

You really know it's time to go when you can't get through a week without upsetting someone with your tone.

*

So, you do it, you make up your mind to resign. Even before you've handed in your notice something changes. You start liking your work again. You start liking the people too. You forget about all the times they've slighted you and talk to them in the kitchen about weekend plans and the football.

You tell yourself you only feel this way because you know you're leaving. It's nostalgia, sort of. It won't last for the next thirty years.

You hand in your notice. The HR manager is surprised but doesn't question it. Her department sets to work drafting your departure email.

You tell your close friends only. Surprised, they ask about the house and money and how you can afford to just quit. You tell them casually, 'We're going to try being poor for a while.'

It's a good line. It feels good saying it.

HR comes back to you. They're ready to press send on your email, inform the whole company of your departure. Are you sure you want to do this though? the manager asks. You seem better of late, talking to colleagues, getting through the work hassle-free. You don't have to quit, you know. It's not always greener on the other side; it's the same artificial grass everywhere.

As you stare at the computer screen and your reply, a feeling swells in your throat, like tonsils full of pus. It tastes about as palatable.

It's pride, a big lump of it.

You've told your friends you don't need this job anymore. You've convinced everyone, including your partner, you're better off without it. You want to prove it. You think you have to.

It's pride and it sticks in the throat.

You send the reply without swallowing.

The email announcing your departure is sent immediately. Only then do you find yourself wondering: What now?

The Root of All Evil

Paul Beckman

The Rabbi enters the ante-room where he trims his beard, adjusts his tallis which he bought in Israel along with the matching yarmulke. They were both bright white and trimmed in bright blue. He squirts breath freshener in his mouth and cleans his rimless glasses then adjusts his expression while looking in the mirror. He grabs his notes and walks out to the bema.

"Please rise as the Belkin family enters and takes their seats."

"Bill Belkin, Harold's eldest, would like to say a few words."

"My Dad will be missed. He already is. He was a proud man. Proud of his four children, proud of his nine grandchildren, proud of his wife, my Mother Tess, and proud of how he built the rickety little building with a half dozen used cars into the largest group of car dealerships in the area. He was proud that he never left for work without a coat and tie and he taught his children to take the same pride in the way we dressed. Dad was proud that he took his wife on only the biggest ships for vacation and always booked a stateroom. If you look at the plaque on the wall next to the Tree of Life you will see that Dad donated this expansion of the synagogue a half-dozen years ago. He was proud of heading the building committee and was involved in every facet of the design and construction. He was a proud man, my father was, and proud that he could leave his business to his children and know that having me as president and my siblings as vice presidents the business would hum along. He planned the 'Say Goodbye to Harold Sale' where everyone who buys a car through the rest of this month gets $1000 cash after the negotiations."

Bill steps down and his mother and siblings rise to hug and kiss him.

The service ends and the Rabbi announces that the family will be first to leave following the coffin. He then tells everyone else to remain in their seats. However, in the back row two men nobody seems to know stand up and walk out the door. One reaches in his jacket pocket and pulls out some papers.

Bill walks out with his mother – his wife and brothers and their families behind them. He walks over to the two men and thanks them for waiting until after the service. One hands him the papers and says, "You're served," and the other says it was a nice eulogy, claps him on the shoulder and says, "pride always before the fall" and they walk off and get in their unmarked police car and drift back to the station and note that Bill's been served the arrest warrants for his and his father's tax evasion. They tell their boss that they can bring Bill in for arraignment at any time but recommend that they wait until the end of the Shiva period. The captain says fine and adds that Bill's father would be proud of how Bill's handling this whole magilla.

Chef's Surprise

Jim Bell

"Eileen, what have you done?" Don's jaw drops in shock. He points at the empty bottle of wine in his hand. "How could you? They are our guests and this is my special night."

Eileen concentrates on mixing a salad. "They are our friends, Don. Relax. It will be fine. Besides, Ann and I like that wine."

Don shakes his head in disbelief. He lets out a sigh and wipes his hands on his apron, the words *Master Chef* emblazoned across his chest.

"I want tonight to be perfect. I've selected a special wine for my meal." He rushes into the dining room. Two couples, all casually dressed, are chatting around the dining room table. A woman swirls her glass of wine as she laughs at a comment. Her husband lifts his glass to his nose. He inhales deeply, savoring the wine's bouquet. He notices Don standing next to him. "Nice apron, buddy," he says with a nod toward the apron's logo. Don takes the glass of wine from his hand.

"I'm sorry. This is not the wine I intend to serve," Don says and continues to collect the filled glasses. The puzzled guests comply with their host's actions.

"I'll bring fresh glasses. I have a more distinctive wine that will complement my meal." Don places the glasses on a tray as the guests exchange quizzical glances.

"Oh, I get it. Don takes our wine, goes into the kitchen, then comes back with the same wine," one guest kids. The others laugh.

"Right, and he wants us to believe it's premier wine," another guest ribs, winking at Don. "Don't worry, Donnie boy. We'll play along."

"Nonsense, you'll find that I serve only the best to my guests," Don says. He kisses his fingers, then opens them like a blooming flower, a gesture of culinary excellence.

Don enters the kitchen with the full tray of glasses. "I'll get my special wine. Where are the other wine glasses?"

Eileen has her back turned to Don as she drizzles dressing on a large bowl of salad. "You're being much too fussy, honey. You never devoted this much attention to a dinner party before."

"I never had time before I retired. Is it so bad I want to show off my new culinary talents to our guests?"

"No, but you haven't been cooking that long, sweetie," Eileen reminds him. "I offered to help."

"Not to worry, Eileen. I have the utmost confidence in my skills. I take pride in my work. Attention to detail is . . ." Don sniffs the air. "What's that smell?" He turns to the stove. "Oh, no, no, no!" he yells as he opens the oven door, then lurches back in horror.

"My Moroccan-roasted vegetables . . ." Don grabs an oven mitt and removes the smoking tray from the oven. The charred veggies hiss at him with disdain.

"Did you set the timer?" Eileen asks.

"Timer?" Don stares at the smoldering vegetables as if he is trying to solve a gruesome murder mystery. His eyes widen as he believes he has found the culprit. He turns to Eileen. "You. Your wine selection threw me off."

"Oh, honey. Preparing a dinner party takes a lot of attention and coordination. No need to be ashamed. It's okay to ask for a little help ..."

"Ah, hah! Caught you again." Don points a finger at Eileen as she samples the chicken he has prepared. "I asked you not to snitch before dinner is served. That chicken is resting. What will our guests think when . . ." Eileen's eyes squint to mere slits as her hand frantically fans the front of her mouth.

"What?" Don asks.

"What spices did you use with this chicken?"

Don points to a cookbook laying on the counter. "Precisely what the recipe calls for. I followed the directions exactly."

Eileen skims over the ingredients as she spits the chicken into her hand. "How much cayenne did you put in?"

Don picks up a tablespoon measure. "One of these, why?"

Eileen tries to ease the upcoming blow. She gently strokes Don's back. "That's too much cayenne pepper, honey. They must have printed a mistake. It happens. You wouldn't know unless you've cooked with cayenne before."

Don snips off a bit of chicken with his fingers and ingests the tiny morsel. His hand darts up and covers his mouth as a muffled "Oh God" escapes through his fingers.

"How am I supposed to know that," Don explodes, throwing his hands in the air. "You would expect someone would proofread their recipes for accuracy. Does no one take pride in their work anymore?" Don leans on the counter with his head in his hands. "My dinner is ruined. And it's not my fault. Not my fault."

"Don't worry, sweetie. I'll take care of everything."

Eileen walks into the dining room. She holds a folded paper in her hands. The two couples are engrossed in conversation about the latest movie release. The discussion fades as four sets of eyes turn to give her their full attention.

"The master chef has decided that, due to circumstances beyond his control, tonight's meal does not meet his high standards," Eileen says. She unfolds the paper to reveal a Chinese menu. "So, who's in the mood for takeout?"

Predators

Mary Krakow

Jacques leaned against the railing and peered into the enclosure. A magnificent lion was attended by three lionesses. Muscles rippled beneath its tawny hide and a breeze rustled its shaggy mane. The only thing that separated Jacques from this lion was a moat. And social norms.

"It's so unfair," he muttered.

A woman looked at him nervously before scurrying with two children in tow to the other side of the viewing area.

Why should the lion get three lionesses to care for its every need when Jacques, who worked out daily and had a full head of jet-black (albeit dyed) hair, couldn't manage to interest a solitary lady? He unconsciously flexed his pecs. Just last night he had postured and roared with the best of them. But the ladies avoided his advances.

He turned his gaze to study the zoo patrons. Women ranging from sixteen to eighty strolled the grounds stopping to admire captive animals. The adrenaline of the hunt heightened his senses. His back to the lions, he rested an elbow on the railing and nodded at prospects as they walked by.

Fifteen minutes passed before his hunt paid off. She was young, maybe twenty, and lithesome. She seemed as fascinated with the lions as he.

"Excuse me. They are magnificent, aren't they?"

"Indeed." She pressed her lips together.

"My name is Jacques."

"Ariadne." She held out her hand.

Long white fingers adorned with blood-red nails tempted Jacques. "Pleased to make your acquaintance." He kissed the back of her hand.

She blushed. "The pleasure is mine."

Jacques' chest swelled with longing. Finally, he had met his match. Or so he hoped. They passed the afternoon together stopping to watch the monkeys' antics and the elephants play. By the time they returned to admire the lions, Jacques' scarf was wrapped around her neck to ward off the winter cold.

Ensnared in his scarf, Ariadne willingly followed him to his flat.

He was gentle, she was yielding.

At month's end they were inseparable—a pride of two.

Jacques visited the zoo daily. He looked with longing at the lion's harem. He turned his back and rested an elbow on the railing, nodding at prospects.

That evening he introduced Ariadne to the newest member of their pride. Like Ariadne, Candice was young, in need of experience.

They purred with pleasure at his touch. Jacques was content.

His two fawning females begged him to sneak them inside the zoo to watch the lions under the stars. Like thieves in the night they crept silently to the lion enclosure. Ariadne unbuttoned Jacques' coat. Candice slipped it off his shoulders. Soon he was naked. He threw back his head and roared.

The lion's answering roar reverberated like thunder inside Jacques' chest.

Ariadne and Candice heeded its call. Together they toppled the naked Jacques into the enclosure where he was soon reduced to bone and gristle.

Heavy Petal

Peter Lingard

When I awoke I sensed my world was going to end and I started to recall my life. I remembered that during my early days I couldn't see outside my protective covers, but could sense the changes in my environment. The world was cool and dark, then warm and light before the temperatures dipped and the dark returned. Juice travelled up my trunk and I felt myself grow and flourish. Breezes cooled me and pleasantly moved me. Swaying in the breeze was the best sensation. Older cousins sharing the same root system sent me messages. They told me that those of us who are most beautiful would be taken and put on show by the Big Beings. According to the last words of those who have gone before, the separation hurts. I knew I, too, would be sad if I had to leave my family. Being together on the common root system made us a happy clan.

Insects came to sit on me, talk to me. There were some who ate part of my outer protection and I worried about how it would affect my appearance. I was infrequently sprayed with a foul liquid that made me want to curl up, but at least it got rid of the eaters. The Big Being that sprayed me also made rumbling noises that I thought might have been addressed to me. They were soothing sounds that made me want to bloom with pride.

One bright time, my protective outer skin started to peel away. It seemed to shed itself and expose me to increasing heat.

My world was getting brighter, too. 'You're very attractive,' a long. hovering insect with double wings told me. I worried he meant I looked appetising, but I appreciated his positive assessment. The Big Being was apparently impressed as well. It sprayed a different liquid; a cool, clean rain on me and flicked away a bug with black dots in his red wings.

The drying, dying layers of my outer protection hung from me and were an annoyance; their weight pulled at my petal base. Their inability to re-cover me made the warmth and brightness more intense and allowed me to haltingly unfold myself somewhat. Big Being came once more and brought the sweet rain; it was a great feeling. The giant tore my now useless protective layers away and although I felt a little tender in the suddenly exposed area I was glad they were gone. Insects with bad intentions kept arriving and I worried I would be eaten before I could fully bloom. Some occasionally nibbled on my outer petals, but the discomfort was bearable and I didn't think they did too much damage. I derived pleasure from hearing them splutter on bits of me that the spray had made distasteful. They so hated the liquid I was mostly spared from their greedy appetites. My goal was to be assessed as beautiful, rather than aid any pollination process like some cousins said I should. Whenever the light faded, I closed my petals and restricted access.

Every time the light started and the source of heat travelled across my world, I raised my head and followed its path, enjoying the warmth and feeling proud. Once a large colourful bird attacked a cousin but we'd already been sprayed and he disgustedly spat out the seeds he'd snatched. The Big Being with the rumbling sounds returned, even though it had already sprayed us. It held something that reflected the bright light. Part of the being took gentle hold of me while the shiny object disappeared below. Then I felt the worst pain. Ooooooh it hurt like I'd been cut in half. It hurt so much I wanted to die. The agony lasted for a long time. I felt liquids leave my body and hoped my wish to perish would be granted. Some of my cousins were cut in half too, and they screamed in pain. I heard a faint, 'you lot need to thistle up' from a malformed, semi-devoured skeleton of a cousin who remained attached to the main stem. We who were in pain were gathered together and taken to a dark, cool place where we were put into something that contained water. What a relief that was. The cool water soothed my wounds and I drank thirstily, hoping to replace the liquids I'd lost.

The quality of the light and dark changed. Throughout what should be the bright time we're shaded, as when the nearby maple tree that I loved shielded us as the source of heat and brightness moved behind her. Alternatively, the dark time is often lit with a cool intensity. I miss the warmth of the brightness, and life has become confusing. The thing that contained us stands on a dark, reflective surface. As I hung over the edge on the container, I could see myself beneath. Big Beings looked at us and seemed to like us.

The light and dark outside have changed many times and I feel more tired every day. My stem has become clogged with the liquid that I have realised contains substances that are not good for me while lacking many that I need. I considered not awakening today, then realised I had no choice. During the dark I felt three of my petals leave me. It was good to have been relieved of their weight but I knew others would soon go and I was incapable of replacing them. When the light came, I saw the petals on the shiny surface below. The sight saddened me and made me realise I was too exhausted to cling on to the life-sucking things. Their beauty had waned with age; their colour faded, and edges withered. Another one detached itself and I realised I'd been withering since the time I was separated from my stem and my tiredness will deepen. I was dying. Did that make me responsible for my petals' demise?

Suddenly, Big Being grabs me and roughly tears away my remaining petals and I know my early-morning premonition was correct. I'm carried to a larger container and shoved head first into a dark, damp, and smelly place. My stem stump snaps as I'm thrust into the depths to join strange and unhealthy-smelling life-forms that I sense are also dying. Then a lid is lowered and all light extinguished.

Exercising Retribution

Jo Hocking

The twenty-something blonde crunched her plastic face into the perfect duck pout. The glossy lips pumped full of collagen puckered like two fat, juicy pink slugs. Her eyelash extensions drooped under heavy black mascara, the colour contrasting against the caked-on nude matte foundation. She scrunched up her long, curly hair. With her head tilted to the left and big doe eyes, she resembled a pug cocking its head for a treat.

Angling her phone like a pro, she snapped a selfie at the exact moment Hannah walked past.

They were the Abbott and Costello of body shapes. In her pink and white Reebok crop top and short shorts, the blonde rocked a set of rock-hard abs protruding like a six-pack of pull-apart bread rolls. Her muscular arms and chiselled shoulders suggested bulk purchases of chicken breast and meal prepping like a boss.

Hannah was a classic pear. She wore a shapeless grey Big W t-shirt that flapped loosely over her bike shorts. A muffin top bulged visibly over the elastic waistband.

"Get out of my shot, you fat cow!" the blonde snapped, returning to her personal Sephora store of cosmetics hogging the shared space by the mirror.

This girl was a fully ordained minister in the religion of fatshaming. Hannah ran to the lockers for her phone and handtowel, then hit the stairwell. She heard the loud snap of an iPhone camera behind her.

On the reception desk upstairs was a huge basket overflowing with a blue-lidded bounty of Head and Shoulders shampoo bottles. A brunette in a Body Works hoodie begged, "Please, take them! We have five pallets out the back!" Hannah grabbed three bottles, wrapping them in her towel.

She walked up the stairs to the weights floor. Music complying with copyright broadcasting regulations but failing the taste test assaulted her ears. Soon, the same Beyoncé track would play at 7:30. Or 7:38 according to the TV clock that never synced with reality.

Hannah seized an empty bench, some dumbbells and worked her meaty triceps.

Suddenly, an offensive miasma of sweat mingled with Lynx Africa descended. A pack of meatheads in Bintang singlets and crotch-hugging compression wear gathered, pointing and leering at someone. One whistled. "Hey, baby! Can I put my face under there?"

One moved slightly, granting Hannah an eyeful of the blonde vigorously squatting with 80 kilograms on the bar. Sticking her knees out, her muscular thighs lifted the weight without the twisted grimace and tennis grunts usually accompanying Hannah's squats. As she stuck out her tight glutes for the guys with a smile, her lack of underwear was as obvious as her love of attention.

A redheaded woman came up to Hannah. "These Insta models are so shallow. Have a look!"

She punched links on her iPhone to reach the Instagram profile of @gymhottieKrystal with 1.2 million followers. It was a bright celebration of ego, avocado, nourish bowls, active wear and quotes undoubtedly screenshotted from Google Images. A perky arse shot demonstrated extreme mastery of reflective surfaces and freakishly good angling. Glamourous selfies in various poses maximised abdominal or sideboob viewing, except for a weird dumpy grey shape. Hannah looked closer. It was a photo of her from behind with the caption: 'Fat girlz don't belong in my gym. Loose some weight! #itsyourownfault #nopride'.

Soul-crushing shame engulfed Hannah as she fled for the second floor cardio room. It was blissfully devoid of people, although the dank stench of body odours and pre-workout fluid was a pungent reminder. Hannah found her favourite treadmill, plugged her headphones in, blared the music and began a consistent waddle on speed 7.

Ten minutes in, she sensed a presence. @gymhottieKrystal was engrossed in her phone as she slung a towel over the neighbouring treadmill. Oblivious to the presence of the victim of her cyberbullying, she jauntily headed to the water fountain.

Girls like Krystal had mercilessly harassed her since she was five. There was only one way to deal with them.

She emphatically hit the red stop button and jumped off, snatching the bottles of Head and Shoulders Supreme Moisture with Argan Crème. Frantically, she shook one like a Formula One winner shaking up a magnum of champagne. Hannah popped the lid and spurted thick white shampoo all over Krystal's treadmill, before gently massaging the most obvious globs in with her towel. Lather and repeat with two more bottles and the treadmill was glossy, radiant and ready to live its best life.

Hannah quickly returned to her machine as Krystal approached, still buried in her phone. She straddled the treadmill, cranked the speed to 13 and jumped on.

Head and Shoulders delivered immediate results. Krystal managed two steps on the selenium slip and slide before she lost her grip and her legs flicked out behind her. Her arms flailed wildly but failed to grab the handrails. Krystal duck faceplanted into the slick surface, her forehead striking a gluggy pool of shampoo with a wet smack. The treadmill roughly launched her on her arse with a thud. Inertia sent her legs backwards straight over her head which struck the carpet, demonstrating that Head and Shoulders really could damage your scalp.

Krystal was a slippery mess of sprawled arms and legs. She raised her head in a daze.

Hannah furiously pounded her phone, uploading a highly entertaining five-second video to Instagram where it immediately gathered more traction than Krystal had managed. She tagged the clip #gymhottiebrokenKrystal and #pridecomesbeforethefall.

She played back the video that was going viral by the sounds of Krystal's madly pinging phone. Krystal went as white as the globs of Argan Crème smeared on her face.

Hannah calmly stated, "This treadmill has been specially formulated to fight the damaging effects of bitchiness. The scientifically proven formula for best results is to avoid contact with this gym because I possess all the active ingredients for your continued humiliation. Now, hit the showers to rinse and do not repeat what you did to me ever again."

Finding Mailman Dante

Ruth Z. Deming

Sitting on the floor, I was finishing my last greeting card when I heard the dreaded thud of my mailbox. Before Dante got the job, I had painted "Hello" on the inside. These mail carriers work so hard and I wanted, if possible, to salute and honor them.

The phone rang. "Don't get it!" I roared to myself. My ninety-six-year-old mother had been ailing. I always think it's the death knell when the phone rings.

Not only was it not her, it was CVS Pharmacy, telling me, on a recorded message, "Ruth, your Novolog is ready." Novolog? I have diabetes and must inject insulin several times a day. I've come to love the looks of the insulin pen. "Live!" it says to me.

I slipped on my comfortable shoes and wool jacket and carried the greeting card like a winning lottery ticket to the mail truck.

Mail truck? What mail truck? It was gone.

One of the complications of diabetes is blindness. Believe me, I'll never get that bad. I did enjoy the film, 'Wait Until Dark' with Audrey Hepburn playing a blind woman. Yes, a proud blind woman.

Pulling my scarf tight around my neck – it was a raw thirty-six degrees – I began my search.

His route never varied. The wind sailed through my mop of grey hair as I walked past the Kiernans' blue house, smelling the Jason Facial Lotion I smear on at night, a mixture like pineapples and mangoes.

A dog barked as I walked up the slope of Greyhorse Road. The wind continued to tease me. And then, to my horror, it blew the letter right out of my hands.

The letter, addressed to my cousin Margie in Solon, Ohio, flung itself like a bird down the street and made a left turn onto Cowbell, my street. My feet, like a tap dancer in *The Red Shoes*, sprang into action, running faster and faster – don't fall, don't fall, I told myself – and then, like a cat pouncing on a mouse, I caught it.

Kissing the letter, oh why not? – I held it up to the sky and thanked God I'd found it.

Now I pumped my legs, I have big leg muscles, though my arms refuse to tone like Michelle Obama's, and raced toward the mail truck. Thankfully, it was standing still.

I ran up waving the letter in my right hand.

I began to cough. Stopped and put my head into my woolen coat with huge black buttons.

Why hadn't I worn a hat?

After catching my breath, I murmured an AA slogan, "Let Go and Let God."

Why murmur it? I shouted it out loud. "Let Go and Let God!"

After all, in the morning when I awake, I go outside to greet the day.

"Hello Neighbors!" I shout. "Have a great day and do something good for your fellow man!"

After capturing my letter, my pink sneakers snuck up to the mail truck, like a thief.

And there he was, sitting inside, oblivious to the world.

He was talking to his girlfriend on his iPhone.

Slipped around to his door, which he slid open.

"Thanks, Dante," I said, thrusting Margie's letter into his hand.

"Have a good one," he said.

And I, proud as an Olympic sprinter, walked home.

The Recent History of the Sánchez Family Tragedies: Part VII

Guilie Castillo Oriard

They tell me at the monastery you've taken a vow of silence and solitude, that you're 'doing penance'. Penance for what? No one seems to know. Maybe they really don't. Maybe they think it's none of my business. (And maybe they're right.) They did say they slip your mail under your door. They don't know if you read it. They seemed rather alarmed at the question, actually.

All this has been good exercise for me, for my memory. I've made peace with things I didn't even know I needed to. I don't blame you for being uncomfortable with this family's history; we all are. Clinging to Maura's fictions, the thin veils of respectability she refused to part even as they grew tattered and ever more transparent, more implausible. When I told your father about the box of Maura's things in Anselmo's workshop, when I spelled out what those documents proved, he still didn't believe it. It creates a crack in one's self, I think, to admit that those one loved have lied, that the reality we took for granted is as solid as quicksand.

And you want to preserve the illusion, too. You can deny us, your family, all you want, but it's precisely this exaggerated sense of pride, the sin at its most corrupt, that marks you indelibly as one of us.

Why does forgiveness come so slow to us, and pride so quick? I often wonder whether the whole thing—Toño being murdered, Anselmo living on the run, a wanted man when he should have been in a nursing home, even a hospice, the rest of the family falling apart, letting first months then years pass between visits, between even calls—might have not happened at all if pride had been left out of the equation. If there had been forgiveness, if someone had said *I'm sorry*, not being facetious or passive-aggressive but really, really meaning it, really wanting not only absolution but clemency. Would the other heart have found its way to the light of mercy, then? Eventually, maybe? Or was there never any hope at all?

We should have seen it coming, I suppose. Two brothers who hated each other living next door to one another at *Villa del Bosque* would be a recipe for disaster in any context. But—actual bloodshed? In a million years, none of us could've imagined that.

I spoke to Anselmo that morning, and he sounded same as he always did. Tired; he had been sick for years, and his hand—he'd lost two fingers in an accident with Toño's chain saw some years before—was paining him more than usual. He complained a little about your father; how he never answered his emails, never returned his calls. Then he told me a funny story he'd read in the paper, and we laughed. I reminded him I'd be by over the weekend to see him, and he said he was looking forward to that.

Did he know then, when we talked, what was coming? Had he already planned it, even? Maybe I flatter myself that I knew him well enough to tell. Or maybe things just ... escalated. We'll never know.

A couple of months later, I got a call from Toño's attorney (the same one Maura had used for her will). He wanted to talk to me, 'run a few things by me,' he said. Apparently Toño had changed his will just a few days before he died, and had designated your father as his sole heir.

But this will, different from the previous one, referred to the whole *Villa del Bosque* property.

"That can't be right," I told him. "Toño only owns— owned—half of *Villa del Bosque*. The other half belongs to—"

"Anselmo, I know," he said. "Or, at least, it did. Up until the day Toño died."

He showed me a document, found at the crime scene (on the kitchen table; Toño was found sprawled on the kitchen floor) and until recently kept in evidence along with everything else the investigators deemed relevant. There was a scattering of tiny darkish spots along one edge of the page, and as I ran my finger over them I realized it was blood. Toño's blood.

"I believe the specialists call it 'cast-off'," the attorney said. "This is only a copy, of course. I've logged in the original at the land registrar."

The document was brief but solidly drafted, and it came to the point quickly: the undersigned, Anselmo Sánchez Haley, hereby relinquishes any claim to the *Villa del Bosque* located at Km. 38 Vieja Carretera a Puebla, San Pedro Nexapa, State of México, México, and further bequeaths any such claims due to him in their entirety to José Antonio Sánchez Haley.

Both had signed and dated the document. The day— night—Toño had died.

This is what I think happened. After years of hemming and hawing about giving Anselmo half of *Villa del Bosque*, as Maura had set out in her will, Toño finally mustered up the balls to take it away outright: if Anselmo agreed to transfer his claim to Toño, he in turn would name your father (and, in his absence, you) as his sole heir. Toño hated his brother, but his brother's son was another matter, and he'd be happy—honored, even— to pass on the property at the time of his death.

Anselmo would have agreed; he had neither the funds nor the energy for a legal battle, he would've seen the logic of Toño's reasoning. He would've also seen the obvious checkmate. (It's a measure of how far Toño had been blinded by hatred—and, yes, also by pride—that *he* didn't.) Anselmo must have asked Toño for proof: *Change your will first, then I'll sign.* How he got Toño to do this I don't know. But once Toño produced the new will, his life was worth a plugged penny. Indeed, to Anselmo, who cared nothing for earthly riches for himself but wanted, more than anything, to do right by his son, now he was worth much, much more dead than alive.

Villa del Bosque is still there, waiting. Your father doesn't want it—predictably, though it still breaks my heart. (As it would've done Anselmo's.) It's up to you, then. Maybe now that you know the whole story, or as much of it as is knowable, you can give Anselmo the happy ending he wanted.

Self-Exposure

Charles David Taylor

He paced around the studio and pondered the shot. Forty-three years as a food photographer, and he'd never done a portrait. Food was his sole *milieu*; people were background, props. But when his biggest client, *Gourmet* magazine, named him "The World's Greatest Living Food Photographer" and proposed mounting a retrospective of his life's work in a well-known New York gallery, he'd agreed to shoot a portrait – of himself.

During negotiations with the editors, it seemed like a worthwhile concession. In exchange for doing the self-portrait and naming the exhibition after the magazine, he'd gained the right to select a significant percentage of his works for the show. Left to the editors, the exhibit would have been only shots from the magazine: *haute cuisine* with famous French chefs smirking behind their prize platters. He'd done dozens and thought such setups a boring cliché.

He imagined the editors' chagrin when he resurrected and mounted the series he'd shot three decades earlier for Dairy Queen. People had questioned his judgment at taking on such a low-brow client – until they saw the work. The artistry of the magnificent eight-foot prints silenced everyone. On his office wall he'd tacked a now-yellowing newspaper article in which an awe-struck writer had risked critic's suicide by comparing his "Chili Dog and Fries" to Caravaggio.

Today he'd sent the staff – assistants, cooks, gofers – home early. He was alone, like in the old days. By eight-thirty, he could no longer delay the inevitable. He stopped at the set: an armless Amish dining chair with a background of light-absorbing black velvet. No distractions, no place to hide.

He was painfully tired. He hadn't slept well for the past five nights and now, at this moment of truth and execution, he moved through a woozy dream-world. His defenses were down, and it was time to set pride aside. He'd made a deal. Anyway, what use was his prized anonymity? Now he must expose himself to the world.

He collapsed onto the chair and looked up, into the big Zeiss lens mounted on his beloved Deardorff. He'd purchased the archaic wooden view camera from a western landscape photographer, a colleague of Ansel Adams. Its 8" x 10" negative had a resolution that no digital camera could begin to match.

He leaned forward, gazing through the fine crystalline glass. The lens elements receded into darkness, like a pathway to infinity – or a tunnel to Hell. He imagined a silent demon at the other end, waiting patiently for prey to venture in. Like a carnivorous plant.

He shook himself back to the moment. He turned on the lights and re-checked exposure with the meter: thirtieth of a second at f/11. He adjusted the lens, watched the delicate blades of the aperture fan out to admit the proper amount of light. His assistant had already adjusted the framing and focus. When she'd asked, "You really want it *that* close?" he laughed. He knew he wasn't pretty.

He withdrew the slide from the film holder and cocked the shutter mechanism. Only a slight press of the bulb in his hand would trip the shutter and expose the film. A mad thought flitted through his mind: *Like a suicide bomber.*

He leaned into position, confronting the lens's glare. And waited for *the moment*.

The curved reflection of his face triggered a flood of memories, like those of a drowning man: how his powerful ambition had crystallized during student days, followed by desperate years of begging for work, enduring the insults and indifference of clients. Then the lucky breaks, but also his shameful subterfuge: how he'd stolen clients from his mentor, followed by the ugly falling out with the old man, who'd been forced into retirement. The guilt. The profound fear of failing. Then success, and guilt was forgotten amid more jobs than he could handle; respect, recognition, mad growth – his own cooks, top-notch assistants, the big studio, schmoozing with big-time clients. Newfound pride and arrogance masking a creeping unease with the shallowness of his craft, a suspicion it was mere trickery.

Deep within the lens was a vacuum of darkness that pulled him in. An old fear chilled his gut, his breathing labored, and at that moment, the demon broke its silence with a beguiling whisper: *That's right, old man – you're nothing but a fraud.*

Instinctively, he pressed the bulb.

A powerful force pulled *something* out of him, and he had a wild impulse to rip out the film and expose it to daylight, convert it to a harmless piece of acetate. But what had been affixed within the light-sensitive molecules of the film was *his self*. Destroying it would be akin to suicide. He had to preserve it.

A few days later, the big negative and its digital scan came back from the lab. He rushed into his office and closed the door, brought up the picture on his massive high-res monitor. At first, shock; but weren't others also horrified to see their own image writ large? He stared, and it passed.

Now he was on familiar ground. For him, the original image – whether an acetate negative or a digital file – was only a starting point. His success was due to his phenomenal skill enhancing an image – blurring, smudging, a thousand tiny adjustments on the way to glossy perfection. In an earlier era, he'd spent days in the darkroom, dodging and burning with precise timing, making print after print until he had *the one*. Now he loaded Lightroom and Photoshop on the Mac, opened the file, and zoomed in.

Too close. He'd lost something.

He zoomed all the way out and took in the landscape of his gaze. The face bore the excruciating weight of years: fear, sadness, self-doubt. But more: obsessive drive, grit, determination, triumph – all was writ upon that face.

Its wholeness struck the eye with full force. He could not, would not alter a single pixel. It was what it was, and what it was, was *him*.

He was done.

The Pink Hotline

Tom Fegan

Ellen Holmes, retired bilingual elementary school teacher, grandmother and widow of a highly decorated Naval Officer, maintained her robust figure through a daily mile walk through the neighborhood. Friends waved and greeted her, in awe of the sixty-five years she didn't resemble. Ellen had grown to love San Antonio, Texas, her late husband's hometown. Alvin was ten years older than she and although it seemed natural he would pass first, his presence was missed. But Alvin was not her only miss; there were her children and grandchildren who lived in other parts of the nation. Visits were almost non-existent.

Ellen kept busy as choir director at St. Mark's Episcopal Church and a participant in the parish Wednesday morning Bible Study. One Wednesday, the Bible Study group was noticeably disturbed. Ellen sat down at the table to listen. One group member handed her a newspaper article.

A male caller referring to himself as "The Pink Hotline" would disrupt a home with obscene messages in the dark morning hours. His modus operandi began first with heavy breathing and then an obscenity-laden snarl. The shortness of the calls and the use of pay phones had made halting the phantom voice almost impossible. Members of the study group were upset. A few had experienced the caller's pranks. The few men present nodded in concern.

"Proverbs 16:18," recited Ellen ecstatically, "Pride goeth before destruction and a haughty spirit falls. Have faith he will be stopped. Now let's study Noah."

A few nights later as she slept, the telephone rang. Ellen rolled over and covered her head with a pillow. But the ringing was incessant. Ellen pushed herself out of bed and glanced at the alarm clock: it was three in the morning!

She sat on the edge of the mattress, thinking of times when the children cried in the middle of the night or were ill with a cold or 'flu or earache. She'd alone had to tend to them: Alvin was away defending the country.

She shuffled to the telephone on the kitchen wall. Her intuition told her it wasn't a family emergency. She guessed The Pink Hotline. She picked up the 'phone, took a quick deep breath and answered, "Hello."

Heavy breathing greeted her. Then a husky male voice spoke, "This is the Pink Hotline. Hey lady, do you want to @#$%!"

Ellen was silent.

"Well?" asked the caller.

Ellen smiled and thinking back to her days as a young mother with a houseful of distressed children, sympathetically cooed, "Oh you poor boy."

The caller slammed the receiver in her ear.

Ellen chuckled and returned to bed, confident that the caller's game had collapsed. Pride had disconnected the Pink Hotline!

The Return of Red Ledbetter
Episode 7: All Together Again

JP Lundstrom

"Not another one!" Detective Red Ledbetter heard the words burst from his partner's mouth. Not for the first time, Leo Wilson exhibited an unpleasant aspect of his personality—envy.

Ledbetter prided himself on being a good cop. His arrest and conviction history was the best in the department. Sympathetic toward victims, thorough in his pursuit of perpetrators, he commanded respect.

It rankled Wilson that Ledbetter was the lead detective. "Another female falls for the Boy Scout detective."

"Leave it. Just get everybody together."

"Get who together?" Had Wilson always dragged his feet, or had he changed?

"Everybody I interviewed." Ledbetter's face was grim.

"What good will that do?" Wilson grumbled.

"You got something to say?"

Wilson shook his head. "No. Let's just get through this so we can go home, all right?"

"Fine."

*

"What's going on?" Sanfte Kätzchen was first to arrive.

"Hello, Miss Kitty." Ledbetter greeted the resident senior citizen.

Belle Charmant followed. "Grand-mère, why are you here? This doesn't involve you."

The older woman's back stiffened. "If there's a crime, of course I am involved, as the Neighborhood Watch."

"More like Busybody Alert," Wilson snorted.

The woman's face reddened, and Ledbetter interceded. "Miss Kitty is a witness."

A booming knock announced Tagata Pe'a, no longer wearing the dragon-bedecked shirt of Chinese delivery.

"You!" cried Miss Kitty.

Another man's bulk filled the doorway.

"My uncle," proclaimed Pe'a.

"Thank you, Tag." Matabang Lalaki, restaurateur, self-proclaimed intellectual, and collector of beautiful things, entered. "Detective, you remember my assistant, Chichu."

The tall, dour woman condescended to nod.

"Out of my way, Spider." As the 'guests' found seats, a small, angry-looking woman pushed Chichu.

"Who's the nutcase?" Wilson muttered.

"I heard that." She poked a finger into Wilson's chest.

"Fiamma Pericolosa." Ledbetter turned to Wilson. "Wife of our first victim, Peter Dick."

"I'm seeking justice for my husband."

"His type always winds up dead in an alley, sooner or later." Wilson's words made the widow's face harden.

"What about my sister, Luz Apagada?" Surprised silence met Tag's question.

Wilson muttered, "Nothing but a—"

"Your sister?" Red interrupted.

"Luz was like a sister to me. She showed me the ropes."

"When my nephew arrived here, he was the soul of naiveté." Lalaki's folded hands rested on his paunch.

Belle patted Tag's hand. "The police will catch her killer."

"They'd better!" Miss Kitty faced Red. "Why are we here, detective?"

Ledbetter watched their faces. "I called you here—"

"*I* called them," Wilson groused.

Shooting Wilson a withering look, Ledbetter continued. "We have here a roomful of persons of interest. Every one of you had a motive."

The stunned individuals exchanged appraising looks.

"Lalaki, you're the kingpin of shady dealings. Peter Dick and Luz Apagada might have known too much, making it necessary to eliminate them."

Lalaki protested, "You have no proof."

"And Chichu, you would do anything for your boss."

"That's my job." She crossed her long legs.

"Tag, you formed a romantic attachment to Luz Apagada. You could have killed them both in a fit of jealousy."

"I would never hurt her," sobbed the big man, "I loved her!"

"Fiamma Pericolosa, your motive is the same as Tag's. Your husband's affair with Luz must have driven you crazy. Did you retaliate?"

The redhead's fire cooled. "Someone beat me to it."

"And you, Miss Kitty." The old woman shrank under his scrutiny. "Besides Miss Charmant, you are related, in one way or another, to every person in this room. You rule your family with an iron hand. Did Mr. Dick and Miss Apagada threaten your control?"

"My late daughter married Lalaki, so he and his nephew are family. My other daughter left me to live in France. Belle and I were only recently reunited. And I adopted dear Fiamma when she was a child. Peter and Luz disgraced the family, but I didn't kill them."

"Then who did?" Belle's eyes flashed. "Why are you throwing accusations around?"

"And you, Miss Charmant." Red's emotionless stare froze her. "Or should I say, *Aimée Amère*? Did the victims know you're not really Miss Kitty's granddaughter?"

"What?" The old lady's face paled.

"Foolish woman," the French girl spat. "Your granddaughter has no interest in you. I took her place to settle a personal score."

"And did you?"

Belle, or Aimée, blew a lock out hair out of her face. "The nature of my revenge was financial, and it has already taken place."

"I'm an old woman!" Miss Kitty wailed. "You can't leave me penniless."

"I have left you just as you left my parents, but I did it legally. I am not a thief." To Ledbetter, she said, "I didn't kill anyone."

"I know that," he said softly. "I apologize to all of you, for having disturbed your night. You'll be gratified to witness the murderer's arrest."

"Who?" They eyed each other, looking for signs of guilt.

"Snowbound as we have been, the shooter has not had an opportunity to remove their weapon from the immediate area."

He turned to his partner. "Isn't that right, Leo?"

"What are you saying?" Wilson's body tensed.

"Pretty convenient that you were the first one on the scene of Peter Dick's murder."

"I heard the call on my car radio," Wilson insisted.

"And then you sent me up to Luz's apartment. You are a good shot—where did you get the high-powered rifle?"

"You need a vacation, Ledbetter—you're not thinking clearly."

"Unless Luz wasn't the intended target. Were you trying to get rid of me?"

"That's crazy!"

"Did Peter Dick get out of hand? Maybe you were afraid Miss Apagada would give you away. We'll find your weapons, and ballistics testing will connect the dots."

"I want a lawyer." Wilson hung his head.

Ledbetter addressed the group. "The rest of you are free to go."

As Wilson was restrained, he accused, "You turned on your partner. I hope you're proud of yourself."

"As a matter of fact, I am."

The storm was over. As Ledbetter left the building, dazzling sun sparkled on the new-fallen snow.

The Blue Ribbon

Steve Carr

Lazzie Monroe felt she deserved a blue ribbon.

Carrying her purse and a small plastic cooler, she passed through the gate and under the State Fair sign. Walking up the aisle between food stands and booths with trinkets, souvenirs and t-shirts, most still in some stage of setting up, she followed the pointed signs aimed toward the Crafts, Baking and Hobbies Pavilion. Once outside it, she took several deep breaths and then walked through the barn door style entryway. Several women in red checkered gingham dresses with white aprons were unfolding metal chairs and sitting them up on AstroTurf that carpeted the entire floor. She sat down in the last row of arranged chairs and placed the cooler in her lap.

"Where is everyone?" she asked one of the women who was setting up the chairs, trying with obvious effort to carry three of them.

"It's still very early," the woman said.

"Not too early for me," Lazzie said, patting the cooler.

The woman walked on.

Four men in denim overalls and wearing straw hats set up long wooden tables along the walls and placed one on a small stage at the front of the rows of chairs. The women who set up the chairs stapled long sheets of white paper to the tops of the tables and tied a different color ribbon to each table end. This was followed by a woman who put on the front of each table a different placard: *pies, cakes, jams and jellies, breads and rolls, table centerpieces, hobby displays, crafts* and *quilts*.

As a few women entered the pavilion and placed their entries on the tables and left, Lazzie rose from her seat and with her purse hanging from her arm, carried the cooler over to the table that read *jams and jellies*. She opened the cooler and took out a jar of dark blue jam. The label on the front read Lazzie's Luscious Blackberry Jam and her full name handwritten on it.

"My jam is going to win this year. I should have won last year, but this is going to be my year," Lizzie said to a woman wearing a light beige pants suit and carrying a clipboard, who was passing on the other side of the tables.

"I'm sure it's delicious. Judging begins in an hour," the woman said and walked on.

Lazzie placed her jar of jam in the middle of the table and left the pavilion.

Leaning against a pole, Lazzie tapped her foot to the rhythm of the calliope music coming from the merry-go-round. Only one child, a little boy with bright red hair and freckles, was on the ride, sitting atop an ornately painted gold and white wooden horse that slid up and down on a metal pole.

"Lazzie Monroe, what are you doing here?" a voice said from behind her.

Lazzie turned. "Hello Hazel," she said. "I've entered my blackberry jam in a contest."

As she straightened her bright yellow straw hat, she said, "So you're going to try again. Good for you!"

"After losing last year to Myrtle Pimroy, I was unable to swallow my pride," Lazzie said. "This year my jam is certain to win the blue ribbon."

"I hope you bring your jam to the next ladies tea," Hazel said.

"It'll be my pleasure," Lazzie said. She glanced at her watch. "I have to go. The judging begins in a few minutes."

Heading back to the pavilion she could feel Hazel's eyes burrowing into her back; news of her entering another contest would spread among the women who attended the teas as soon as Hazel could get to a phone.

In a chair as near to the stage as she could get, Lazzie nervously played with the snap on her purse. The judges, two women and one man, dressed in costume versions of farm folk, complete with bonnets on the women and a straw hat on the man, stood behind the table on the stage, each with a handful of white plastic spoons in one hand.

The judges opened the jars of jellies first and placed them in a row. One by one they lifted a jar, sniffed it, and then put a spoonful in their mouth. When the jelly in all eight jars had been tasted by all three judges, they turned their backs to the audience for several minutes, and then turned around.

"The blue ribbon winner of this year's jelly is Sue Crafton's Strawberry Sunrise," the male judge said. He then placed the small blue ribbon on the jar of jelly.

A woman in a bright orange angora sweater several rows back let out an excited squeal.

The audience of thirty clapped excitedly.

As one of the female judges opened the jars of jams, Lazzie bit her lower lip.

The judges each scooped up a handful of new plastic spoons and began smelling and tasting the jams.

When they were finished tasting and after talking and had turned back to the audience, Lazzie grinned broadly, certain she would win the blue ribbon.

The male judge said, "The blue ribbon winner of this year's jam is Lazzie Monroe's Lazzie's Luscious Blackberry Jam." He placed the ribbon on the jar.

The clapping of the audience thundered in Lazzie's ears.

With her purse hanging from her arm, and holding the empty cooler in the other, Lazzie walked into her house and closed the door behind her. She walked through the silence of her home into her kitchen. She put the cooler on the sink counter next to an empty jar of Drake's Blackberry Jam. She took the jar and sat down at the table, opened her purse and took out the blue ribbon. She placed it on the empty jar.

Victoria Seizes the Reins

Larry Lefkowitz

A radio 'books' program invited both Victoria and myself to be jointly interviewed as "Lieberman's closest associates" (she as the late critic's wife, me as his right hand), as the radio hostess generously put it when introducing us to her listeners. Victoria managed to take over the lion's share of commentary. She seemed guided by the tactics that the more I looked bad, the better she would look. She hinted that I was a dabbler, a dilettante, as opposed to Lieberman, even though it was I she had chosen to complete Lieberman's unfinished book.

She then launched into a spiel about all the sparkle, wit, and wisdom that Lieberman brought to the book, then mentioning (in dismissive coda) my "editing" of it. Not content with disparaging my herculean contribution to the book, she turned to ad hominem attack, bringing up what she denigrated as my "cheapness" (Nitza, my ex-wife, had used "parsimony", I preferred "frugality"), that I insisted on walking whenever we went anywhere together – even here (to the studio – it was true), never taking a cab (she wouldn't hear of taking a bus). I did not rejoin that Victoria lamented the passing of the sedan chair. And when the radio hostess asked her at one point, "To which moment in your life would you like to return?" assuming, perhaps, she would mention some brilliant harp recital or an endearing moment with her late husband, Victoria paused significantly before answering, "To the moment before I met Kunzman."

I should have been on guard from the moment I first saw her in the studio. (Victoria had *glided* into it, in marked contrast to my own halting ingress, uncomfortable with the whole idea of an interview, let alone a joint interview with Victoria in which she would engage in her favorite topic – herself.) She was dressed in what I thought of as her "Henry VIII mode" in which she summoned up the combination of splendor and menace found in the famous Holbein portrait of Henry VIII, conveyed best in the expression, 'Dressed up to kill.' And I knew that during the studio interview to come Victoria would be capable of providing information which was in part true, in part imagined, and in part fabricated, intermixed with bouts of false enthusiasm punctuated by her overly robust, operatic laugh.

Victoria had embraced me, not out of affection, but as a means of whispering in my ear, "Kunzman, remember that the public does not want to hear about *you*, but to hear about Lieberman."

As I was digesting this remark, she added, "I hope you won't be unpleasant."

"You think I'm unpleasant?" I challenged her.

"Don't think about it too much," she replied.

"*Nu?*" I persisted, stung by her suggestion, even though I suspected that it might have been a deliberate tactic on her part to put me on the defensive.

"Mildly pleasant," she replied. "At times. On occasion." After a pause, "On this occasion, I hope."

Victoria employed her pauses even more significantly during the interview. A shtick of hers, taken, I assumed, from the Yiddish theatre which she liked to attend, so that every word of hers that went out over the airways would be significant, with me her hoped-for silent partner. I was reminded, however unlikely the comparison, of St. Teresa, who kept a stenographer at her side so that comments from her ecstasies would always be suitable for publication. Victoria had ecstasies of her own.

My pauses were usually induced by a lack of something to say on my part or a failure to respond to some snide remark on Victoria's part directed toward, or about, me – for instance: "Say something profound, Kunzman" or "Kunzman is the consummate scribe." She meant to Lieberman. Did the listeners grasp this or, hopefully, think she was praising him? As I wrestled with these possibilities, Victoria had moved on to providing free psychoanalysis of me over the airwaves, "Kunzman's problem is that he wants everyone to be *nice to* him. That's why he writes." Oddly, Lieberman once said something to the same effect. Sometimes Victoria seized on a pause of mine to begin and continue with one of her spiels, though her favored tactic was, again, the barb. "Kunzman is thinking. Kunzman likes to think. Other people breathe. Kunzman thinks."

At other times Victoria employed to good effect her machine-gun speech when angry or determined to make her point, potent verbal weapons which covered up her at times shaky assertions. "Kunzman doesn't realize that telling is enough, explaining, too much." Not bad, I thought, though offended. Less successful, perhaps, her "All Kunzman does is read, write, and read." Pause, then, "Kunzman spends too much time in his own head. Even when he sleeps." At this latter hint of contiguity, I blushed – the radio listeners couldn't see it, and I hoped the interviewer didn't notice, but I was sure Victoria noticed. On one hand, her hint at physical contact between us would fly in the face of her All-Lieberman stance; on the other, it fit her dramatic love to shock. Stung by her sallies, I left off such musing and shot back, "There is hardly enough interview time at my disposal to succeed in portraying all the nuances of behavior and peccadilloes of the Lady *(here I nodded at Victoria, despite the radio audience's inability to see it)*, though 'nuances' is too nuanced a word to apply to her." She didn't know whether I was praising her or defaming her, but suspecting the latter, lashed into me.

Victoria: "Kunzman is so touchy."

Kunzman: "Me? Touchy?"

Victoria: "You. Touchy. Like now."

During our mutual review (in theory – she monopolized most of the time) I received a number of cold stares from Victoria whenever I said something less than praiseworthy in her eyes.

I was relieved when the interview was over. Victoria seemed triumphant. Even the interviewer bestowed on me a pitying glance as she shook my hand after it was over.

Woodhouse Moor

Nod Ghosh

Steve
How can I forget the moment I began to love you less?

I'd just gone down on you. I was waiting for reciprocation, but you turned away.

"Shelley, can you – you know – "

I guided your hand towards me.

You pulled away, complained of a hangover.

"Too many beers. Too many goodbyes." You slipped out of bed, left me aching, just as you had the night before. Your insistence that people mustn't know about us was wearing me down.

I considered jerking off, but the thought made me feel small. It wasn't going to happen. You'd cast me aside like a spent match.

Again.

I pulled my clothes on, lit a cigarette and slipped out without a goodbye.

Hannah
The Saturday it happened, I'd known something good was coming.

The Saturday it happened, I was meeting friends at the Royal Park. That's where Steve drank. He'd smiled and said hello the last time.

The Saturday it happened, I'd made a special effort. There was a fragrance in the air. *Possibility.*

I'd found a dress at the charity shop. Black velvet and lace. It reached my ankles. I wore the leather boots Mum had given me for Christmas, and smudged kohl around my eyes, blood red lipstick. A hideously expensive pendant from *Boodle Am.*

The woman staring at me from the mirror looked like someone else, someone elegant, alluring. Something swelled inside.

I'd met Shelley's friend Steve a while back, but we'd only spoken once or twice, crippled by the incoherence that comes with desire. Sometimes there is a longing that goes beyond words.

The Saturday it happened, Steve walked backwards into me, and we'd started talking. Two beers had loosened my tongue, my confidence boosted by what I'd seen in the mirror earlier.

That was the Saturday we went to a party. That was the Saturday we kissed, the maddening scent of spring driving our passion. Music throbbed and hummed around us like blood.

That was the Saturday I wound my arms around him, felt the muscles in his back tense and relax as he worked his lips over mine. Pulsing.

That was the Saturday I understood I was good. I was special. I was the best.

It happened when Steve whispered, "I've waited a long time for this, Hannah."

Steve

Hannah and I bumped into each other at the Royal Park the night before you went away the first time, Shelley. She took me to a party. There was madness in the air. Everyone was in love, including me. But you'd taken me for granted. You paid a price to chase your dreams.

I started seeing Hannah. Her devotion eclipsed my doubts. I felt it when she touched my face, her love when she said my name. She made it sound like poetry.

We'd walk hand-in-hand on Woodhouse Moor.

Hannah took me to an art gallery and for once in my life I understood what it was about. Did we ever do anything like that, Shelley?

Those first weeks were wonderful. Yet I kept thinking about you.

Then I lied to Hannah and ruined everything.

We'd been together for a month, long enough to let our guard down. Long enough to have lain in each other's arms all night without sex, just holding each other because we couldn't let go.

The lie slipped out under the cover of darkness. We were making out in the open. That isolated part of the moor near the allotments where people grew potatoes and dumped broken fridges. That place with statues of the Duke of Wellington and Victorian industrialists, covered in graffiti. A late spring sky with no moonlight, the call of drunks and distant fire engines the only sounds beyond our gasping and moaning.

"I want you." The huskiness of my voice clarified my intensions.

"Out here?" she asked.

"Yes. Now."

I slipped my hand out from under her clothes, reached into my pocket.

"I can't find – I've left my, you know. You got any?"

"No." She sighed and squeezed me.

I groaned. "We could chance it."

"Not a safe time." Her mouth was saying one thing, her hand another.

The steel of my erection guided my actions. "Statistically speaking, the chances – "

"We can't." She pulled away. I could have screamed.

"Hannah." I brushed my finger on her cheek.

"Hmm?"

"I've come to realise I love you." My lie slipped out, but oh, it had the desired effect. She couldn't see my face. She didn't hear my hesitation. She didn't know I was imagining your softness against my fingertips, not hers. Darkness covered everything.

"I love you too," she said, feverishly covering me in kisses.

She let me fuck her. Hard and fast. Caution seeped into the ground beneath us like spilt milk. The green smell of crushed grass compounded my lie with its false sweetness. I thought about you, Shelley, wondered when you'd be back.

Hannah

It lasted two months.

"I can't handle this," Steve had said.

He'd caught me by surprise.

"Handle what?"

"This. Us."

"Did I do something wrong?"

"It's not you. It's me."

The cliché burned like scalding vinegar.

He walked away.

He didn't say goodbye.

Steve

Shelley, you've often asked why I went back to Hannah when you went away again. You have despised my wife over the years, even though the two of you were once friends.

I would have come back to you if you'd asked. But you never did. Not until it was too late. Not until there was someone else to consider apart from Hannah and me. We married in haste, as people did back then.

We shouldn't have.

You see, Shelley, there was a moment all those years ago when I started to love you a little less. Hannah slipped into that moment.

But I never stopped loving you. I never will.

Hannah

They say every sin has a price.

Steve

I kiss you. A silent hand leads me from your stone-cold lips.

All seven stories written by Nod Ghosh for the *7 Deadly Sins* project are adapted from the unpublished novel *The Iris Tattoo*. Nod Ghosh completed this work with support from the New Zealand Society of Authors Mentorship scheme, with Norman Bilbrough as mentor, in 2015.

My Final Testament

Chris Hall

I am a humble man who has spent his life in servitude, providing for others and devoting my energies attending to their needs and fostering their welfare. I am ambitious and have achieved much, and am proud of those achievements that have served the public good and allowed many to fulfil their own life ambitions.

I myself have lived a happy and fulfilling life, and now, as it draws to a close, I have to tell you, I am very pleased with my personal accomplishments. Many men saunter through their life without purpose. They merely meander from one hedonistic venture to another. But not me, oh no, I set myself a goal from a very early age and never veered from my path.

For this very reason the gates to the kingdom of heaven will be flung open upon my approach. St Peter will warmly greet me with open arms, as I have been his model subject. One that God can be very proud of.

I set about establishing my business straight out of school. By the time I was 21, I was already a millionaire, but that was just the start. I employed hundreds, and then thousands of people, providing them with the opportunity to earn a living and feed their families. I was their saviour. Everyone looked up to me and I repaid them with boundless opportunities.

I was awarded many honours, and deserved every one of them. I was afforded a god-like status within my community, and deserved every last accolade.

I gave to charities and funded humanitarian projects. I warrant a special place in heaven at God's right hand, because He will never again be afforded the opportunity to have someone as pure and virtuous as me to serve Him.

He will be proud of me like no other before or after.

Balancing Cheques

Pat O'Connor

People looked up to me because I had been a bank manager when bank manager was something to be. Not like these days, with everything centralized and computerized, and electronic transfers from peoples' phones. Give me a cheque book any day. A cheque book is a solid entity. You keep it in the inside pocket of your jacket, do your reconciliations on the stubs, and you always know exactly where you are. When my expert advice is required, as it occasionally is by solicitors, auditors, etc., that is what I tell them: use a cheque.

So when this carefree run-a-job fellow fixed my slates and wanted cash, naturally I demurred.

"A cheque or nothing," I told him flatly. "Who should I make it out to?"

"Charles Ulysses Cumming," he said, hanging his head. Because now, you see, he had to put it through the books. Pay tax etc. I signed the cheque with my Cross fountain pen.

"Oh boy, that's one bee-u-tiful pen, boss! Can I see…?"

Of course with his big hoary fingers, he dropped the blasted pen, and nearly crunched it with his clumpy boots. I had to scramble round the floor after it, and oh such a fuss. I couldn't wait to get rid of that simpleton, and reconcile the amount left in my account: £25,254.

Imagine my shock when I got the monthly statement, to find that a cheque for £25,200 to C.U. Cumming had been cashed right after the £150 cheque for Charles Ulysses Cumming. The cheque numbers were three apart. I immediately pulled out my chequebook, and sure enough, after two unused cheques, the third cheque was missing, the stub not filled in. I could not breathe, or sit upright. Automatically, I clambered for the phone, to contact the police, the bank, anybody.

Then I thought... oh my god, I'll be a laughing stock! My money was gone, and if I had any experience of such matters, I knew I would never get it back, even if they caught the bastard. All I could hope for was to save my reputation, and to do that I had to keep quiet.

And that is what I did. Although from then onward, if anyone asked for banking advice I felt sick inside. I felt that my standing had fallen, and I could not shake the awful suspicion that everyone knew what had happened.

But when I was asked once again to give my expert opinion in a matter of alleged cheque fraud, I realized that no, everyone did not know. My secret was safe. And so it was with relief, even a degree of elation, that I agreed to give an opinion in the case, but only after ascertaining that the offending party was a plumber, a Mr N. Sterling, not C.U. Cumming.

Upon entering the courtroom, the first person I saw in the front row was C.U. Cumming, his rough coppery head grinning brazenly at me. I was transfixed. Of course it was my chance to tell all, to demonstrate how even *I* had been hoodwinked, and damn the fellow to prison. An usher, noticing my unsteady condition, led me to a seat, and when I was called to give my opinion, I stammered and stuttered to the effect that it was not possible, if a cheque was properly written, to change it from twelve pounds to twelve hundred pounds, which was what this "plumber", Nick Sterling, had on the invoice that the complainant denied receiving. I could not meet the eyes of anyone in that courtroom.

Awash with nausea, I staggered out to a washroom to splash my face, and retreated home.

For weeks I refused invitations, pleading tummy upset. But after a month of no further developments, normality seemed reestablished, and it was the day for the Rotary Club lunch. So I donned the three-piece suit, and peeped out the front door. All clear. I was about to step forth when I noticed in the postbox a brown envelope with hand-scrawled address. I opened it with forensic delicacy. It contained a letter requesting donations for a charity supporting alcoholic ex-prisoners. My initial reaction was – Ha! Buying them drink, more like! But the letter was accompanied by a photocopy of two cheques – my missing cheque, and the one I had signed. In a trance-like state, I re-read the letter. It was signed Robin Gently, and it recommended I set up a modest standing order from my bank account. For convenience.

The Parable of the Bread

Lia Lewis

As every good Orthodox Christian knows, prosphoro (leavened bread given out during Holy Communion) is made with these simple ingredients: water, flour, yeast, and salt. Also, what every good Orthodox Christian knows is that this bread is usually made by sweet little old ladies.

But the town of Claremount is very different. In Claremount at St. Theodore's Greek Orthodox Church, the little old ladies used to bake the bread for Sunday services. For many years now, Yianni Pappas has baked it because everyone including Yianni knows his prosphoro is the best. Yianni is a middle-aged, pious Orthodox Christian who is unmarried. Yianni's baking talents are well known at St. Theodore's. He not only bakes bread but he also bakes a mean cupcake.

Fr. James, the parish priest, encourages his parishioners to donate their time and talent and Yianni listens to Fr. James. Since Yianni knows he's the best, then he's sure to win favor with Fr. James and the rest of the parish. In order for him to make sure he's noticed, Yianni never fails to mention his prosphoro baking prowess every single Sunday at coffee hour. He is so proud of himself that his pride blasts like a beacon on a foggy night.

One day, though, Yianni had a heart attack and died. (Maybe it was all those cupcakes?) Fr. James was saddened because not only did he lose a valued member of his parish but also who was going to bake the prosphoro for next Sunday's service? And would it be as good as Yianni's? The old ladies were sad because they'd have to pick up the slack now that Yianni died. They were enjoying their retirement. But on the upside, the parish was happy that they'd never again have to listen to Yianni brag about his baking prowess.

But Yianni's story doesn't end here. It seems that when he died, he didn't quite make it to St. Peter's Pearly Gates but ended up in a beautiful industrialized kitchen with all modern conveniences where he's the head baker as well as all the assistant bakers. His task is to bake the leavened bread for church every Sunday. But when he removes the bread from the oven, he doesn't find the perfect golden brown, chewy bread as per the recipe. He finds a flattened, gray blob. He sighs and puts it aside and starts all over again, hoping that the next loaf will be perfect. He never understands what the problem is because no matter what he does, the bread never bakes the right way.

Hospice

Norman Klein

I got out of my car reminding myself not to let my ex, Lorna, get to me. It was just like her, a snail-mailed request for a visit written in bold black ink, and the reason in larger gold letters. 'We must set things straight with the children,' it said. My first thought was that the children were in their forties, old enough to muddle through, then I realized it had to be something serious that I didn't know about.

The day after the black and gold mail came, an email from Lorna warned me that the front door had been nailed shut. I was to come to the back door, give a shout, and let myself in, which I did.

"Sorry, Greg, it sticks a bit doesn't it? Just like this damned recliner," Lorna said.

"I love the new window. Nice view of the gardens," I said.

"Remember this recliner?" she asked, pushing the hand pedal to raise herself upright.

"Was it your father's?" I asked.

"No, it was yours. I gave it to you for your birthday and you threw it in the garage and covered it with a tarp. That's right, I haven't seen you in ten years, have I?" she said.

"Maybe more," I said.

"Well, anyway, thanks for coming. And don't worry I'm not going to ask you for money."

"Good, but I will take you to lunch if you're up to it."

"I'm not. That's why I asked you to come. I'm dying. Did Andrea tell you? She wasn't supposed to, but I knew she would, now that she's living with you."

"She told me two years ago."

"That was just a close call. How is she doing, by the way? I'm worried about her."

"So am I. She has two jobs, and she can't sleep at night. She worries about you, and by the way, she wants you to call her."

"Tell her I will when I know more."

"More about what?"

"Finding a hospice."

Lorna had experienced several false alarms in the last five years. The last one began with a twelve-hour operation and ended with two setbacks and a week in London with her lawyer friend.

I waited for her to tell me how long she had, but she wouldn't say.

"So what's going on with the children, Lorna? What's this about?"

"It's about the will. Rick says I'm under water, but Andrea says if she sells the house I would get enough for the hospice and the rest would pay for the work she's had done on the house for the past ten years."

"Sounds good. So what's the problem?"

"When I last spoke with Rick I told him a will had been written, and he asked if his children would be provided for. I didn't take it seriously. You know how he is. I thought it was his way of telling me he didn't believe I was dying."

"I talked to Rick on his birthday. He said he and Bob were thinking of adopting a child. Maybe two."

"But not right away. They can't afford it," she said.

She had told Rick she had only weeks to live, and that Andrea had her power of attorney.

"Rick called to tell me your lawyer wanted to set up a trust that would have me owning the house and paying the mortgage until the house was sold," I said.

"It's fine with me. I don't care. I know nothing about it," Lorna said.

"Sounds like the same lawyer who represented you when we split."

"So, what's wrong with that?" she asked.

"Never mind, that's water under the bridge. The will is signed. Andrea is your executor."

"True, Andrea needs to be executor to protect her interests," Lorna said.

"I agree. Andrea has to come first, because she's dead broke," I said.

"But that reminds me, Greg. There is one thing you can do for me. It's the Delft Blue. I want you take it away and hide it, because some day she'll want it. I know she will."

"Will do," I said, glad there was something I could do for her.

"Greg, do you remember our little talk twelve years ago, just before you announced your engagement to what's her face?"

"I think so. You told me you had become a Christian Scientist."

"Well, I'm not sure any more. Lately I've been more a Unitarian Universalist. If I die tomorrow, tell Andrea that."

"Will do," I said, hoping that was the end of her list.

"Thanks, Greg, and here's one final thing. The most important thing of all really. I would like you to deliver my eulogy."

"No, Lorna, the kids should do that," I said.

"I've already asked. Neither of them will do it. I have some notes here, things to say and not say."

"Could I see them?" I asked.

"No, not until you promise me."

"Why not let your lawyer do it?"

"He can't. His wife would kill him."

"Okay, here's a suggestion. I'll pay Andrea to do it, but the funeral will be by invitation only."

"If that's the case, I'll ask her not to invite you or my lawyer," Lorna said looking out her window.

The Beauty of a Vacation

Annabelle Baptista

"Gucci purses!" Evaline said, and veered away from the Cannes boardwalk, away from the sounds of the speedboats, the rocking yachts docked in the harbor and the people sitting in boardwalk cafés chatting over umbrella drinks. She climbed the slope to a vendor sitting under a tree with ten bags of different sizes and colors. He held up a tan bag, trimmed in gold with an embossed Gucci buckle.

"I've always wanted a Gucci purse. How much is this one?" Evaline took the gold and tan bag from the young man's brown hands and felt the buckle, then modelled it over her shoulder.

"For you, beautiful lady, one hundred dollars."

The young man had African features and flawless skin. He was tall, yet slight. His shirtless chest achingly defined bone by bone as if he wore a cage.

"A hundred dollars is too much," she said. She shook her head and looked at the other purses, but she had her mind made up for the one she was holding. She tested the zipper, pulling the slider up and down its teeth and yanking at the stitching. He looked like a nice young man, about eighteen. He wore baggie khaki shorts and a half-a-heart pendant chain around his neck.

Walter was slower than Evaline, but soon he was standing beside her snorting at the bags as if they smelled of rotten fish.

He bent down, picked up a bag, and threw it back on the pile dismissively.

"Don't waste our money. Can't you see this is just a scheme, a ripoff. Don't always be so naïve. You can't get something for nothing."

"They're not giving them away, Walter." Evaline rolled her eyes at him, then turned to the young man. "Fifty," she said, shaking the bag. She could carry this purse among the rich and famous on the boardwalk.

"For you, beautiful lady, sixty dollars. All styles, for you the same price." He gestured over the handbags.

"Are you crazy," Walter countered, "come on Evaline, don't be ridiculous. These are counterfeit. I've heard of the police stopping people at customs for counterfeit merchandise."

Evaline batted his hand away.

"We're in Cannes, Walter. I want to walk the red carpet and have my picture taken with the khaki and gold Gucci purse," Evaline's voice cracked. "Don't always deny me the things I want." She imagined herself wearing it out for an evening concert when they got back home. She would call Lydia Mullen and propose the idea.

Walter didn't like concerts. She'd surprised him with the vacation plan. The money she had saved from working as a logistics clerk for a large firm for forty years. She had been around the world a million times in her imagination, sitting at her desk in Colorado and proofing customs documents for containers travelling overseas.

Finally, she'd managed to convince Walter to rent a car and travel through the south of France. But his presence was like a dark cloud on such a bright and clear day.

"Do you know how long I had to work to earn sixty dollars? We're retired, it's not like we have a money tree."

Evaline handed the young man fifty dollars. "That's all I have," she said.

He took it. "Beautiful lady, you have made a wonderful choice, you have a real Gucci bag, now."

He pulled a newer purse still in plastic out of a deflated duffle bag. The other vendors were now close enough to hawk their wares.

"See, you are an easy mark and they know it," Walter said and pulled her away, batting at the young boys as if they were flies.

"What a beautiful bag," Evaline said, taking it out of its plastic as they returned to their stroll on the boardwalk. Walter had his arm hooked on hers.

On closer inspection she saw the "U" in Gucci was broken. Still, it glistened like the half-a-heart chain that hung around the young man's neck.

Evelyn uncoupled her arm from Walter's.

"You don't have any faith in people, Walter. That's what's wrong with you! Maybe he will use the money to go to college," Evaline said, stuffing the plastic inside the bag she now carried on her shoulder.

"Don't bet on it," Walter said.

"You get what you give," Evaline said, swiping a silver curl behind her ear.

The Tyrant's Garden

Aaron Retz

"No, I can't sell you that one either," said the man, with a wave of his pruning shears.

"Why?" I asked.

"It's quite perfect. I couldn't possibly part with that one."

First there had been the sick one, which *looked* perfectly healthy, but apparently needed to be nurtured back to health before it could be sold. Then the one that was too old and dear to him, and another that reminded him of his first true love.

"Hey man, do you want to sell me a bonsai or not?"

"Maybe come back next week," he said, his eyelids drooping with disinterest.

I couldn't resist going back to see what this guy's story was. He wasn't in the garage, so I poked around and was tempted to leave some cash and take off with one of his bonsai. But through a nearby door I heard a noise.

He stood at a small pond crowded with splashing goldfish. He was feeding the fish, his back turned, tossing out flakes that fluttered to the silvery surface. Around the pond four stone ledges formed a tight amphitheatre, with dozens of bonsai neatly lined along each concentric plane. The mother lode! Surely one of these would be up for grabs.

"Hello there, Mr Bonsai. I'm back."

"I was wondering if you'd return," he said, his back still turned, feeding the fish. "So you really want one of my trees. Or maybe you just came out of curiosity." He was wearing the same heavy, grey shirt and pants as last time. He looked like a mechanic.

"I admit you're a curious fellow."

He turned. "Well, I still don't have one to sell you."

"Why do you even have a sign out front?" I said. "Is this a business or are you back here just having a laugh?"

"Ha! I am fond of laughter, particularly when people come in here telling me how much they love bonsai and start waving their money in my face."

"So you really don't sell these things?"

"Occasionally, if I feel it will end up in a good home." For a few moments there was only the sound of the pond pump, humming.

"What's a good home?"

"I have always believed in tough love," he said. "It doesn't necessarily work on humans, but these tiny trees have no option but to obey me. *They do not do their own thing.* Sometimes they try; sometimes they get sick. But the weak ones are disposed of if they don't quickly recover. And each species has its own natural form and tendencies—this counts for something, *but not a lot*. Precise control of the shape and size of every healthy specimen is my singular purpose, each one a mirror reflecting the unique quality of my soul."

"You should consider getting out more buddy," I said, shaking my head. "They're just little trees."

He closed his eyes and breathed deeply in an obvious effort to stay calm.

"Yes, my friend. They are *just little trees*. And *you* by the same measure are *just a little human*."

"Okay, last chance for a sale," I said, reaching for my wallet.

"Young people today are convinced they have something important to say, but they don't. They should bite their tongue and learn to listen, like these *little* trees. I will tell you what a good home looks like! It's one in which all leaves tremble, as if in the presence of God. Are you prepared to instil unspeakable fear in these pathetic plants, as I do? Can you tame and master nature with your vision, with your bare hands?"

I looked around and shrugged my shoulders.

He threw out more fish food and dismissed me with a derisive wave. "I didn't think so."

As I walked back through the garage I liberated two of his bonsai and hurried to my car, possessed by a strange combination of fear and delight.

Also from Pure Slush Books

https://pureslush.com/store/

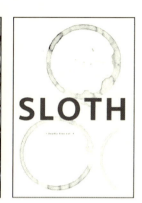

- Envy 7 Deadly Sins Vol. 6
ISBN: 978-1-925536-70-6 (paperback) / 978-1-925536-71-3 (eBook)
- Wrath 7 Deadly Sins Vol. 5
ISBN: 978-1-925536-68-3 (paperback) / 978-1-925536-69-0 (eBook)
- Sloth 7 Deadly Sins Vol. 4
ISBN: 978-1-925536-66-9 (paperback) / 978-1-925536-67-6 (eBook)
- Greed 7 Deadly Sins Vol. 3
ISBN: 978-1-925536-64-5 (paperback) / 978-1-925536-65-2 (eBook)
- Gluttony 7 Deadly Sins Vol. 2
ISBN: 978-1-925536-54-6 (paperback) / 978-1-925536-55-3 (eBook)
- Lust 7 Deadly Sins Vol. 1
ISBN: 978-1-925536-47-8 (paperback) / 978-1-925536-48-5 (eBook)